JI

D0312782

WITHDRAWN

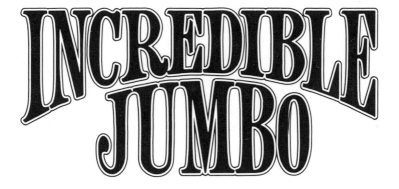

A Novel

BARBARA SMUCKER

VIKING

SAN BRUNO PUBLIC LIBRARY

VIKING
Published by the Penguin Group
Penguin Books Canada Ltd, 2801 John Street, Markham, Ontario,
Canada L3R 1B4
Penguin Books Ltd, 27 Wrights Lane, London W8 5TZ, England
Viking Penguin Inc., 40 West 23rd Street, New York, New York
10010, USA
Penguin Books Australia Ltd, Ringwood, Victoria, Australia
Penguin Books (NZ) Ltd, 182-190 Wairau Road, Auckland 10,
New Zealand

Penguin Books Ltd, Registered Offices: Harmondsworth,
Middlesex, England

First published 1990

1 3 5 7 9 10 8 6 4 2

Copyright © Barbara Smucker, 1990

All rights reserved. Without limiting the rights under copyright
reserved above, no part of this publication may be reproduced,
stored in or introduced into a retrieval system, or transmitted in
any form or by any means (electronic, mechanical, photocopying,
recording or otherwise), without the prior written permission of
both the copyright owner and the above publisher of this book.

Printed and bound in the United States of America
on acid free paper ∞

Canadian Cataloguing in Publication Data

Smucker, Barbara, 1915-
Incredible Jumbo

ISBN 0-670-82970-6

1. Jumbo (Elephant) - Juvenile fiction. I. Title.

PS8537.M82I62 1990   jC813'.54   C89-095240-X
PZ7.S6648 In 1990

British Library Cataloguing in Publication Data Available
American Library of Congress Cataloguing in Publication Data
Available

*For my husband Donovan
who likes elephants, zoos and circuses
as much as I do.*

ACKNOWLEDGEMENTS

Special thanks to Wayne Franzen, elephant trainer and head of Franzen Brothers Circus, for an interview at his winter headquarters in Webster, Florida; to Jenny Wallenda of the famous aerialist circus family, who has retired in Sarasota, Florida and who informed me of many circus happenings; for the fine collection of materials on Jumbo in the St Thomas, Ontario, Public Library and for the impressive Jumbo monument located at the west entrance to this city; for interviews with Heidi Epp of Richmond, British Columbia who is also known as "Bubbles" the clown; and to my editor, David Kilgour, for his sensitive understanding of an elephant and a boy and how to tell their story.

INCREDIBLE JUMBO

PART I

1

A boiling African sun sank slowly into the sea. It blazed blood red for an instant and then scattered into a glitter of gold as it slid under the waters of the Indian Ocean.

The gold light focused on an elephant family of twelve huddled around a towering mother with long, straight tusks.

It was a solemn moment. An hour before, she had given birth to a perfectly formed baby calf. The new mother's head drooped and her legs sagged; she had carried this baby inside her for almost two years.

An aunt touched the little male calf with the two sensitive "fingers" at the end of her trunk. She seemed to approve of his three-foot height, his 250-pound weight, his hairy, reddish brown body and his toothpick tusks.

The baby tottered on his tree-stump legs. He squinted at his family with his small eyes, then took a brash step forward. His feet splayed out in four directions, like a table with legs of jelly, and he landed on his belly. An older sister gave him a push upward with her front foot.

Another aunt snorted her approval, showing perhaps that she thought him to be very bold.

A brother squealed as he sucked up dry dust and sand with his trunk and blew it upward over his back. The flies and mosquitoes that buzzed around him were quickly smothered. He looked skyward and shook his head. The new baby seemed to him downright foolish.

But the new baby wasn't watching. He began to tangle with the four thousand tiny muscles of his amazing trunk. He threw his trunk over his head. He swished it back and forth. Finally, he stuck the tip of it into his mouth and began sucking it as a human baby would suck his thumb.

His oldest aunt's monstrous ears flapped and swished as she watched the young calf's silliness. She gave him a gentle shove with her trunk toward his mother's front legs.

At once the new baby seemed to know what to do. He flung the bothersome trunk over his head and began to suckle his mother's milk with his mouth.

The family watched patiently, touching the new baby gently now and then with their trunks. They would all help take care of him—three aunts, two grandmothers, an older sister, two brothers and four lively cousins. The baby's father was not there. He roamed the grasslands and forests alone.

One of the grandmothers stood apart from the family circle. She was older, wiser and larger than the others; she was their leader, the matriarch. There was nobility in the lift of her massive head and strength in her arched back. But her tusks were chipped, and one was broken. She was the first to use her tusks to dig roots, to bore holes for water, to break branches, to strip bark. She was the first to protect her family. Once, she had pierced the body of a lion who tried to attack a small elephant calf.

There were not many wild creatures in Africa who would dare to attack the largest land animal in the world. Only lions and crocodiles sometimes tried to defy an elephant.

But there were other dangerous enemies in the grasslands and forests—men. Men had a strange scent and their movements were sly, never predictable.

Danger seemed far away on this golden sunset evening. The elephant family was content. They intertwined their trunks with one another and shuffled into a protective circle around the new mother and her baby. The arrival of a new calf was a time for celebration.

Then, without warning, the matriarch began kicking up dust with her forelegs. Her trunk shot upward, twisting and probing the air in all directions as she sniffed for scents of neighbouring elephants and for strange and foreboding smells of danger. The adults lifted their trunks in unison to join her, swaying them rhythmically back and forth like signal flags. They could catch scents as far away as two miles.

A harsh trumpeting noise of alarm blasted from the matriarch's trunk. Her ears spread wide like cupped sails. The new baby huddled close to his mother's protecting legs.

The scent of danger was strong. Elephant sounds for "men" passed among the family. Flies and mosquitoes swarmed in menacing circles and the wide flapping wings of blackbirds spread foreboding shadows.

Then slowly, very slowly, the matriarch lowered her trunk. The fearful scents had disappeared, but the matriarch's spreading ears were still stretched out wide and alert.

The exhausted new mother relaxed. She leaned against the trunk of a large acacia tree, closed her eyes and dozed. Her baby kept on filling himself with milk.

A male cousin sniffed at the baby with mischief in his eyes. This baby was a big eater. Then he rubbed his trunk lovingly over the little calf's back.

Eating obsessed all the elephants. Their lives were one long meal, both day and night. To fill their giant bodies, the grown-ups ate at least 350 pounds of shrubs, plants, fruit and bark each day. Eating took them sixteen hours a day.

The sister and brothers of the baby calf began

to tear up bunches of tall grass, beat them
against their knees to clean them and then stuff
them bit by bit into their mouths. It would not
take long before all the tall grass around and
under them would be eaten.

Through the long night, some of the family
ate while others took short naps, some standing
and others lying on their sides. By the time
morning came they were all thirsty and walked
to the nearby river. Every grown-up elephant
needed fifty gallons of water each day.

During the night, the baby calf had gained
strength and could walk with the others, but he
stayed safely by his mother.

As the family ambled down a dusty path to
the water, the baby calf's eyes blinked with wonder. The elephants weren't the only creatures
here. Bucks of all kinds also gathered beside the
river. Baboons lumbered along the shore; blue
monkeys jumped through the trees; an elegant
giraffe appeared with her endless pole of a
neck. And, sitting in front of them on the opposite bank of the splashing river, guarding a salt
lick, was an enormous rhinoceros with small
eyes and a horned nose. He charged at the new
mother.

She was in no mood for such behaviour.
Pushing her baby gently to one side, she
plunged through the shallow water toward the
beast. Her strong trunk curled around his middle and she flipped the startled animal off his

feet into the deep water. He flailed his ungainly
limbs in the waves and swam to the opposite
shore.

The aunts and grandmothers swayed back
and forth and then ambled joyfully into the
water. The mischievous younger elephants
plunged into the river squealing with glee, shov-
ing and showering one another with water from
their trunks. All of them were expert swimmers.

The new baby wanted to join them, but first
he needed a drink. Again, his trunk was a problem. He held the tip of it out of the water and
tried drinking with his mouth. Finally he
watched his mother sucking up water with her
trunk and squirting it into her mouth. He tried
to imitate her and found that he could do it.

Time passed with the rising and the setting of
the sun, and there was no counting of days or
months or years to measure it. The elephant
baby grew stronger and larger. He was almost as
big as his brothers and much bolder. He had
play fights with his cousins, trumpeting loudly,
raising his flapping ears, intertwining his trunk
with theirs and pushing them backwards into
the thorn bushes. His mother had to stop him
sometimes by giving him a whack with her
trunk.

There came a year when the African sun
steamed with furious heat. It seared the earth
day after day until all the grasslands where the

elephant family roamed were parched and all the green leaves were shrivelled. Even the water in the river disappeared. The elephants dipped the ends of their trunks into the dust, then shoved the earth aside with their feet. The only water was buried deep inside the earth, and it had to be sucked up in dribbles. The elephant family was desperate.

One night the matriarch trumpeted an alarm to elephant families nearby. They came trumpeting and shuffling on their round, padded feet until a herd of some hundred elephants had gathered. With dry mouths and empty stomachs they milled around the matriarch. Her wise old eyes lingered on their wasted baggy hides, and then she lowered her head and swung her massive legs towards the west. The extended family of a hundred followed in single file. The growing baby marched closely beside his mother.

They tramped with steady rhythm, pounding the earth into wide packed roads, knocking down trees with their battering-ram heads, crunching and chewing every living branch and every green leaf.

Finally, one day dark clouds blew into the sky and a blessed rain fell on the starving herd. It splashed into the dry river bed beside them and they stood along its bank drinking greedily. The rain did not stop. It poured into the river and foamed into swirling rapids.

The rushing, tumbling water fascinated the young elephants, especially the daring calf, for he was the boldest and most mischievous of them all. He rushed to the wet, slippery bank without caution. The soft earth crumbled under the weight of his feet and he crashed over the side like a tumbling boulder. He splashed with such force into the water that his mother felt the spray in her eyes.

The screams of the young calf sent his mother following him with lightning speed above the bank, until she came to a low spot and could wade and then plunge into the fast-rising torrent beside him. The current pressed the terrified calf against her side. They bobbed along together like immense floating corks.

Farther and farther they floated until they could no longer see any other elephants. They crashed against twisted branches and now and then touched the jaws of crocodiles. There were hours of tossing and buffeting until the river narrowed. The mother swung her trunk around the large branch of a tree and pushed against her calf until he landed on the shore. She pulled herself after him.

They stood close together, dripping and shaking, on a strange wooded shore without any scent of elephants or any sign of elephant paths. There was only the paralysing scent of men everywhere.

The mother rolled down her trunk and flared

out her ears. It made her look twice her size. A high-pitched, urgent scream blew from her trunk. Such trumpeting would surely frighten any enemy. But her stance against danger had no effect in this land inhabited by men.

A gunshot sounded from behind a tree and a small silver bullet flew through the air. The mother could do nothing to stop it. There was no brave defence that she could mount against this deadly pellet. It pierced her head just above her ear and entered her brain. Her mountainous strength was no match against this man-made weapon. Her back legs toppled and her trunk reached upward like the neck of a proud giraffe. Then she collapsed. She was dead.

Hunters emerged from behind the tree and came running. The long, straight tusks of ivory from this giant elephant would sell for high prices.

The calf tugged and pushed against his mother, pulling at her awkwardly pointed tusks and her crumpled legs. He tried to lift her head. He cried and moaned until a strong net of fibre was thrown over him. For the first time in his life, the bold young calf could not move.

2

Men now seemed to appear from everywhere. They surrounded the young elephant calf. He knew at once from their foreign scent and their strange behaviour and their chattering noises that they were the creatures who had frightened his grandmother, the matriarch. Now they had somehow made his mother fall into a lifeless heap on the ground, and they had bound him in a way unknown to wild animals. He was enraged.

The angry, confused young calf had never known real fear until he fell into the flooded river. Then, his mother had rescued him. Why didn't she rescue him now? He was too young to know about death. A low rumble rose from his throat. It was a moan of distress.

The hands of men reached through the heavy net that bound the calf. They tied thick ropes around his hind legs and then his forelegs and they looped the rope around the trunk of a sturdy tree. They pulled the binding blanket of fibres from his body.

The struggling, bewildered elephant swung his freed trunk into the air and trumpeted shrilly. He threw the weight of his body against the tree but it wouldn't bend, and his new growing tusks were too short to pierce and slash at its trunk. His bound feet were useless. In his fury he flapped out his ears to their full size.

"This elephant has a fiery spirit," one of the hunters said. "I'd guess he's four or five years old, but he's strong and bold for his age."

"It'll take a long time to tame him," his hunting companion laughed. "There's no fear in his angry little eyes. I think I'll call him Bold One."

The newly named Bold One did not know or care what these creatures thought about or called him. He kept on tugging and pulling and trumpeting wildly. His throat grew dry and the blazing African sun that beat down on his back added to his ravenous thirst.

Suddenly a bucket of water appeared in front of him and he plunged his trunk into it as though his life were at stake. He sucked up all the water he could hold and squirted it gratefully into his mouth. Another bucket appeared. This time Bold One filled his trunk and aimed it in the opposite direction, spraying the water with all his strength into the faces of the men around him.

They spluttered and fumed. "Maybe hunger

will calm you down!"

Bold One was starving and there was nothing to eat as far as his trunk could reach in all directions. Until now, his closely knit family had always given him food and drink and loving protection. Now they were gone. Tears fell from his eyes. He became frantic, thinking of his mother slumped on the ground. Surely she would rise and come to him and tear away the binding ropes, and they would walk together back over the elephant paths to the forests and their family. He sniffed the air again and again for her scent, stretching each muscle in his trunk to its limit. But there was no scent at all of elephants in the breeze that blew above him.

Night came. Buckets of water were placed around Bold One, but no food. His skin seemed to fall about him in folds like some great tattered cloak. A little of the defiance inside him began ebbing away. His trunk dangled listlessly from his bowed head. He could think of nothing but food.

Finally in the cool early morning one of the hunters walked near the starving young elephant and held out something in his hand. The hungry calf looked up wearily. His stomach ached and rumbled with hunger. He gathered all his strength and banged his body against the tree and swung his trunk angrily at the binding ropes around his feet. This man had caused his misery.

Then his swinging trunk stopped in mid-air. It caught the delicious scent of wild raspberries and black plums, the most luscious-tasting fruit in all of Africa. They were in the man's hand. The young elephant lifted his trunk cautiously, grabbed the fruit and threw all of it into his mouth. He squinted sideways at the hunter, who winked at him and walked away.

The man came back, and this time he threw a pile of dried grass at the elephant's feet. Without caution, Bold One ate mouthful after mouthful until every blade was gone. He was still hungry. But he was beginning to know that this man would bring him food, and when he appeared again Bold One no longer wanted to trample him or grab him around the waist and toss him into the lake.

Bold One now had food and water, but his feet were still shackled and his mother had not come. He called loudly for her with long, plead-ing cries. A dark cloud seemed to circle around him and he floated in and out of the real world and his jumbled memories.

Was he dreaming when, early one morning, the ropes were untied from his feet and then quickly looped over his neck? At first his feet stayed rooted to the ground. Then he discov-ered that he could shuffle them back and forth. He cautiously lifted one after the other and started to run, but the rope yanked at his neck and choked him. The men behind him prodded his hind legs with sharp sticks. He could do nothing but go where they pulled and pushed him.

The hunters and Bold One began tramping day after day through strange lands of glistening lakes and vibrant foliage and then strips of barren desert and steaming sun. The young elephant yearned for his mother. But he felt strength return to his growing legs. It was good to swing them freely and it was better than standing with shackled feet. Here and there were fresh leaves and green grass for him to eat. One evening he smelled something new, something salty—the Atlantic Ocean. The hunters led him along its shore near a dock where noisy, bustling men raced in and out of great sailing ships like busy ants.

Bold One was prodded again by sticks and forced into a box attached to a pulley. It had one small opening for his trunk and head to stick through. There was a tug and a pull and the box with the elephant inside was hoisted into the air. The young elephant's stomach twisted and turned somersaults, and his body banged backwards and forwards. There was no experience he could compare with the terror of this flying box. It sailed downward and then landed with a thud on the deck of a ship.

After a dizzy moment, Bold One opened his eyes and discovered that there were many other

terrified animals around him. There was a
rhinoceros, a giraffe, three monkeys, two zebras
and a cage of chirping birds. They were stacked
together in various boxes on the ship's deck.
Bold One could feel the ship moving. A sea
journey began, a horror of rocking waves and
violent winds.

Then one day the ship remained still and
Bold One smelled land. He trumpeted loudly.
Could this be the end of the nightmare journey
through splashing water that he could not
touch or drink? He tried lifting his trunk to
catch the scent of his strong, proud mother. But
his packing box remained tightly closed. It
swooped into the air and this time dropped into
the freight car of a French train heading for the
city of Paris. Soon there was a roaring rumble of
wheels and a clatter of bumping train cars. It
was dark and the baby elephant could not see
or hear his frightened companions, the
rhinoceros, giraffe, monkeys, zebra and birds.
At the end of two days this terror ended, and
Bold One and the other animals were taken to a
big park in Paris, called the Garden of Plants. It
was both a zoo and a garden.

Released at last from his box, Bold One tottered fearfully into a large, sturdy cage. Four
large elephants lowered their heads and stared
at him. Were they really elephants? Their scent
was different. How could he know that they
were elephants from Asia, with smaller bodies,

smaller ears and one "finger" instead of two on the tip of their trunks? He didn't like their long, narrow faces. Two of them were without tusks and the other two had only little ones. His mother's tusks were long, smooth and straight and gleamed in the sun.

Sunsets and sunrises came and went unnoticed by the young elephant. He was lonely and unhappy. At feeding time the four big elephants got most of the hay and boiled potatoes. There was no sky above him and no trees or leaves to swish against his trunk and no one who could replace his mother. He still needed her.

Months passed. Bold One could not get used to this place. The managers of the zoo decided that he should be exchanged for a rhinoceros and sent to another zoo. There was a second terrifying seasick journey for him.

This time the unhappy elephant had no will or strength to protest being shoved into another shipping box. He had no desire to stand or swing his trunk. He closed his eyes and fell against the side of his box. When the swaying ship anchored at last, a loud cry announced his destination—"Regent's Park, Royal Zoological Gardens." The year was 1865, and Bold One, now seven years old, had arrived in London, England.

Men pulled him from his box with ropes and laid him in a room on a concrete floor. A tall, white-haired man came into the room and looked down at the feverish, unconscious elephant. His name was A.C. Bartlett and he was the superintendent of the zoo. He tipped his tall silk hat, straightened the tails of his frock coat and pulled thoughtfully at his long, white beard. Then he knelt on the floor, recklessly ignoring his fine clothes, and gently rubbed the forehead of the newest arrival at the Royal Zoological Gardens.

"Call Matthew Scott at once!" he said sharply to a waiting attendant. "If anyone can help this sick, ill-kept animal, Scotty can."

The superintendent stayed on his knees studying young Bold One.

"Under all this sagging skin and dirt," he shook his head sadly, "I think there is a fine specimen for our zoo's first African elephant."

He ran his hands down Bold One's limp but sturdy legs. His eyes were furrowed with concern, for he was a man who loved animals. He was dedicated to the zoo and to the scientific scholars who had founded it. He saw each new animal as a special gift needing expert treatment and constant care.

Mr Bartlett lifted Bold One's trunk and scooped some water into his mouth.

"An African elephant must have an African name," he pondered aloud. "I think I remember hearing a Swahili word that means chief or something large. . . . Was it Jumbi? . . . Ah! That's it! We will call this elephant *Jumbo*!"

A stocky middle-aged man dressed in the drab blue uniform of a zoo keeper hurried into the room.

"So the African elephant has come?" He was excited. Then he looked closely at the dirty, sick creature lying on the floor.

"Oh, the poor thing," he knelt beside Mr Bartlett and began stroking the back of the young elephant with his rough, sturdy hands.

Mr Bartlett rose to his feet.

"I am assigning the full care of this elephant to you, Scotty. Spend all of your time with him if necessary." He moved towards the door. "Call me at once if you need help. I'll check on both of you later. And by the way, I have named him Jumbo."

Scotty would have wanted the job of caring for this elephant even if it hadn't been offered to him.

"Come now, cheer up." He smoothed the wrinkled forehead between Jumbo's eyes.

The newly named Jumbo blinked one eye and then slowly opened both of them. The dream he was having of his mother faded in and out until it began to be replaced by the image of this kind-looking man beside him.

Jumbo looked at the perky waxed moustache on the man's face, and the bowler hat that curled up around the edges and perched at the back of the keeper's head. Jumbo stretched out his legs, hoping that they might also be rubbed.

Scotty brought a tub of warm water and a soft brush and began scrubbing away the clotted dirt and matted insects that covered Jumbo's skin. He cleaned the scrapes and bruises on his back and legs with healing ointment. He trimmed the twisted toenails that would have been worn away by walking if Jumbo were in the wild.

Jumbo watched with wary eyes, but when the keeper spooned oatmeal and warm milk into his mouth, he feebly lifted his trunk and stroked the man's arm.

"You and I will make a team," the keeper said. "Everything is going to be just fine for you, Jumbo."

Jumbo closed his eyes for the first peaceful sleep he had had since he had last seen his mother.

3

When Jumbo woke, Scotty was gone and he was alone. It was dark outside and the new scents and sounds of the great city of London throbbed around him. He felt clean and stronger. He wanted to swing his giant legs, plough through some tangled jungle and pump blood through the miles of vessels in his growing body, or thrust his trunk upward as far as it would go. But there were walls all around him. He shrieked loudly against this binding suffocation.

Then he heard his cries mingle with the wild night cries around him—the roar of a lion and the chattering of monkeys—that echoed through the zoo, and he felt a little comforted as he had sometimes at the zoo in Paris. He also heard the shuffle of elephants nearby, but they had the same scent as the four unfriendly elephants who had shared his cage in Paris.

He banged his foot against one of the walls, expecting sharp pain from his ingrown toenails.

Nothing hurt and then he remembered the man with the curling moustache who had soothed and cleaned his itching skin, who had spooned warm milk into his mouth, who had cut away the stabbing toenails. He would wait for this man to come again.

Jumbo swept up some scattered hay with his trunk and munched it with more vigour than he had shown for many months. And, with the first streak of daylight, Scotty did appear. He was followed by a thin, surly boy who tugged at a bag of hay. Jumbo backed away from this new man-creature.

"Open the bag and scatter the hay on the floor, Turner," Scotty ordered gruffly. Then he approached Jumbo and his voice became gentle. It was a well-known fact at the zoo that Scotty's love and affection were reserved for the animals, not for the people around him.

"Good laddy, good Jumbo," Scotty repeated over and over again, stroking the elephant's trunk.

Jumbo relaxed. He liked this attention from the man who had bathed his sore hide.

But who was the other man-creature with the shabby jacket and worn shoes and sneering face? Jumbo thought of charging at him. But the sight and smell of the fresh hay that the boy was scattering on the floor overwhelmed him. His stomach rumbled with hunger. He forgot the man-creature who now had backed away from him and stood watching from a corner of the elephant paddock. Buckets of water appeared and he sucked them up and swallowed in gulps.

"This is going to be a lively, healthy, fast-growing elephant," Scotty mused, pulling at his chin. He turned to the boy, Turner.

"I'll tie a rope around his neck and take him for a walk along the paths before the visitors begin to arrive. You shovel up the dung, Turner, and be sure you scrub the room neat and tidy while we're gone."

Turner kicked at the dirt-covered floor and mumbled to himself, "Filthy beast—clumsy-footed monster."

Jumbo saw the rope and backed away from it. Ropes had been tied around his feet until he couldn't move and squeezed around his neck until he couldn't breathe. Scotty understood. Caring for animals had been his life-work.

He boasted to the other keepers, "Elephants are the smartest animals in the zoo, but they don't know their own strength. They could smash a man to death just by leaning against him. They need to be trained the minute they come into our Gardens. That's why they need me."

Mr Bartlett and Scotty were rigid about animal-training rules. None of the ancient methods of terrifying an animal into submission—such as the cruel use of red-hot irons—were ever allowed.

"Each animal is a separate personality," Scotty explained to those in awe of his success. "You 'ave to be strict and then you 'ave to be kind. You get to be friends and you trust each other."

Scotty handed a carrot to the suspicious Jumbo, who munched it quickly and reached for another. This time Scotty slipped the rope around the elephant's head and led him out of the Elephant House into the bright sunshine.

Jumbo sniffed the air and trumpeted softly. His feet felt the soft earth. His trunk collected the mingled scents of roses, geraniums, dahlias, catmint and yellow snapdragons from the many carefully tended flowerbeds. They intoxicated him, and he jumped into a small lumbering dance, catching Scotty off guard.

Jumbo had to learn at once that he had to be orderly and calm while strolling through the Gardens.

"You can't be steppin' on a body's foot with your hoppin' and your skippin'," Scotty told Jumbo, pulling more tightly on the rope and nudging his left front foot with a long wooden bull-hook which he carried.

But as they turned a corner, the sweeping branch of a willow scraped over Jumbo's back and the leaves tickled his sensitive skin. Fresh leaves! Jumbo veered from the path towards the tree. He remembered the luscious taste of leaves in the forests of Africa and he remembered how his grandmother, the matriarch, had torn down the branches to eat them.

"No Jumbo. No! No!" Scotty shouted sternly but without anger. He pulled the rope again and prodded with the bull-hook, guiding Jumbo back to the path. He handed him another carrot.

Jumbo munched at the carrot and shuffled his feet faster, following Scotty until they came to what looked like a hole through the ground. Jumbo stopped abruptly in front of it.

"It's a tunnel," Scotty began chatting in an easy-going way as though Jumbo could understand. "It's nothing to be afraid of. It leads from our part of the zoo, under the Outer Circle and into more of the Gardens. The lions, the camels, the monkeys, the bears and the seals all live on the other side."

He started slowly walking through the richly carved entrance. Jumbo edged close to Scotty and followed him. When they passed through the darkness and into the light, Jumbo turned around as if he wanted to try it again.

Back at the Elephant House, Turner splashed water over the floor and swept most of the debris into a corner. He was a sweeper and cleaner at the zoo and had been tugging his buckets and brushes from cage to cage since he was ten. Now he was older and slightly bigger and ready for easier jobs and better pay. There were no such jobs around. But he was sly. He knew how to catch buns and treats that were thrown to the animals of the zoo and slip them into his large jacket pocket. It was rumoured that he had skills as a pickpocket, but he'd never been caught. Complaints about his slovenly work came from animal keepers. As a last resort he was assigned to Scotty.

"He's an orphan and Mr Bartlett is keen on helping him," a zoo supervisor told Scotty. "Shape the homeless lad up, Mr Scott, or he'll be out on the streets with the beggars."

There was a knock at the door of the Elephant House and Turner opened it. A man came in to deliver Jumbo's lunch—a bucket of oats, more hay, three loaves of bread, three cabbages and eight apples. Turner pocketed five apples and a loaf of bread, and threw the food quickly into a corner. He was about to leave when Scotty and Jumbo came in the half-open door.

Scotty looked about quickly and stormed over the half-washed floor and carelessly scattered food. He stood over Turner with his long-handled bull-hook and supervised another cleaning.

Jumbo flapped his large ears and ambled at once to the pile of food. Within minutes it was gone.

4

J umbo soon began to adjust to his quarters. They were now cleaned with a bit more care by the begrudging Turner. The elephant's physical condition improved, and he walked with swinging steps when Scotty took him for his early morning tours of the Gardens. He also became bold, playful and mischievous—the way he had been when he was a baby in the African forests with his family. Mr Bartlett noticed this one day on his regular visit to the Elephant House.

"He's like a child in the hospital who is getting better," he said to Scotty. "He's beginning to show off and be disobedient. He's even a little rough."

Jumbo threw a loaf of bread into the superintendent's face.

Scotty was shocked. He and Mr Bartlett had talked about the dangers that could develop when a fast-growing animal like Jumbo had to learn to live in the small quarters of the zoo.

"The keeper in charge of Jumbo," Mr Bartlett spoke softly, "must be his master and control his behaviour. Jumbo doesn't know his own enormous strength."

Scotty agreed.

The two men grabbed Jumbo by the ears and gave him a swift thrashing. The young elephant lay down on the floor and bellowed a cry of remorse.

"He's telling us that he's sorry," Scotty said. He looked at Jumbo with affection and handed him a carrot.

One morning as Jumbo and Scotty were returning from their morning stroll, they noticed unusual activity at the Elephant House. The keeper of the bears ran to meet them.

"Did you know," he said with such excitement that his eyes bulged, "Bartlett has purchased a new African elephant? Her name is Alice. She's to be housed next door to Jumbo!"

Scotty quieted him, for he already knew about the new arrival. But Jumbo smelled the scent of an elephant from Africa and he bellowed loudly. His memory could flash instant mental pictures to him of his mother, his grandmother, his brothers and his sister.

But when the two elephants met through the bars of their cages, the visitors and staff were disappointed. The two elephants looked at each other, sniffed and turned away. A newspaper story tried to link their names together romantically. But Jumbo preferred the company of Scotty and the children who came to the zoo.

"Alice doesn't seem to like people," Scotty decided, "and Jumbo does."

Jumbo was now the favourite animal in the zoo and the boys and girls shouted, "Jumbo! Jumbo!" whenever they saw him. He began to grow quickly.

"He's becoming a moving mountain!" Mr Bartlett exclaimed.

Jumbo grew as tall as the door of his house—almost eleven feet tall. His feet spread out as large and round as giant drums. He became too heavy to mingle freely with the children in the Gardens. Scotty put him in an outdoor enclosure where buns and treats could be fed to him through the tall iron fence that surrounded it.

Jumbo was also becoming a celebrity. Famous people came to look at him and Scotty's pride in being his keeper showed in the special tilt of his new bowler hat. He discarded the drab uniform of a zoo keeper for a bright new pepper-and-salt suit.

One day Scotty announced to Mr Bartlett that Jumbo needed a larger room and better care and that he especially needed a new sweeper and cleaner. He even wanted someone to operate a stall nearby where fresh buns could be sold just for Jumbo.

"Turner is a dour fellow with no pride in his work," he told Mr Bartlett. "He scowls at Jumbo and Jumbo scowls at 'im. He's no longer a boy. He's a grown man."

"But we have kept him from becoming a beggar and a thief," Mr Bartlett smiled. "Where could we move him, Scott?"

Scotty had an instant answer. "I think what I'd do," he said, "I'd send 'im to work with that ugly beast, Obaysch the hippopotamus. 'is Arab keeper from the Nile can't speak the King's English. Turner could at least talk for 'im . . . the two of them are meant for each other. They both 'ave bad tempers."

"That might just be the answer," Mr Bartlett mused.

He then began to review with Scotty the applications for jobs in the zoo that had been brought to his attention. He seemed especially interested in a mother and son who found themselves in poverty when the circus where they were working was destroyed by fire and the father of the family was killed.

"Circus!" Scotty exploded. "There's no relation between our zoo and a circus."

"I've talked with them, Scott," Mr Bartlett continued. "Molly Tolliver was the circus school teacher, and the young boy, Tod, took a great interest in the circus menagerie. He was especially fond of a little elephant from India."

Scotty became interested. "How old is the lad?" he asked.

"I think he said ten. He's small and thin for his age, but he's wiry."

"Well," said Scotty slowly. "I think we could give 'im a try."

A few days later Scotty met both Tod and his mother. The boy did seem small, but his eyes were lively and he had an eagerness about him that Scotty liked. He also was impressed with the mother. She's a real lady, he thought to himself.

The following week, Tod Tolliver appeared for work at the Elephant House. His thin, freckled face was scrubbed until it glowed and his stiff brown hair had been freshly cut in such straight lines that it made a frame about his head.

Tod shivered and Scotty noticed the clean but skimpy clothes that covered him. He handed the boy the smallest sweeper's uniform that he could find and then pointed to his pail and brooms.

"I was a sweeper and a cleaner for the circus, Mr Scott," Tod said. "I know just what to do. But, please, may I see Jumbo first?"

Scotty led him to the outdoor enclosure where the elephant was swinging his trunk between the rails of his fence for buns.

"Oh Mr Scott," said Tod. "I will love him. I know I will."

Scotty and Jumbo left soon for their morning stroll, and Tod Tolliver scrubbed and swept Jumbo's quarters until they gleamed like a

gentleman's lodgings. Then he turned four
perfect cartwheels and was about to do more
when there was a knock at the door. It was the
man delivering Jumbo's lunch.

After the man left, Tod neatly arranged
Jumbo's food in one corner and then quickly
broke off the end of one of the loaves and ate
it. He stuffed an apple into his pocket. He
wasn't stealing food from Jumbo, he argued
with himself, for his pay as a sweeper would
barely cover the rent for the shabby room
where he lived with his mother. They had sel-
dom had enough to eat since leaving the circus.
How could he take care of this fine new elephant unless he, too, had food inside him?

Tod's mother was practical about it when he
took half a loaf of bread and a red apple home
to her.

"The elephant won't miss it, Toddy," she
smiled at him. "You can pay him back with extra
care and cleaning."

Tod looked at his mother and smiled back.
With Mr Scott's help she had just been hired to
run a stall near the Elephant House where she
would sell buns and apples. Now they would
have two small salaries instead of one and they
could buy all their own food.

The buns that Tod's mother would sell were
to be fed only to the elephants and especially to
Jumbo. Scotty had demanded this. Such jobs
usually went to the zoo keepers' wives, but

Scotty had no wife and no family and he had been impressed by Molly. He liked her good manners, he told Tod.

"She's a proud lady, too," Scotty added.

Tod agreed silently. Scotty was right. Many times his mother had told him how she had fallen in love with his father, who was a circus clown. When she married him, her family had cut her off without a penny.

"My mum was the teacher for all the circus children when we were on the road, until my father died in the fire," Tod said aloud. He decided not to tell Scotty that he hoped to be a circus clown like his father, and that he practised cartwheels and somersaults whenever he could.

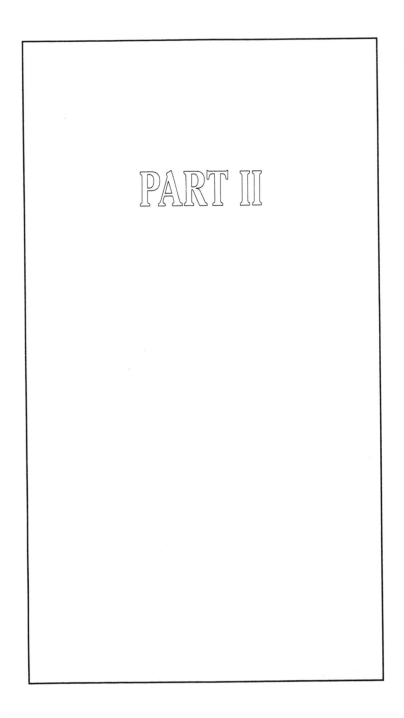

PART II

5

Jumbo no longer felt trapped and bewildered. He had found a home and a keeper and a family, this time among friendly men. They had given him a new name that he knew belonged just to him. There were other names that he knew—Bartlett, Scotty and Tod.

On the Sunday that Molly was to start her new job at the Zoological Gardens, Tod woke before daylight. He didn't make a sound as he pulled on his freshly patched knickers and clean worsted shirt. He clamped his cap down tightly over his newly cut hair and then ate his cold gruel without even a sipping noise.

His mother needed an extra hour's sleep, for she had done a day's washing the night before and would deliver it on her way to the zoo. The money helped pay for some of their food. Tod was about to leave when a harsh screech of twisting wood shook the room. Molly woke at once and stumbled to the window with Tod. They looked down at the creaking boards that covered their outer wall. The wall seemed to sway towards the dirty, narrow street below.

"Oh, Toddy," Molly shivered and wrapped her worn shawl around her shoulders. "I'll not have us losing our lives over rotting wood." She began coughing hoarsely and reached for a bottle of ugly dark liquid.

She grabbed Tod and hugged him as he started for the door a second time. "It's like a marvellous dream to think that I have a job in the London Zoological Gardens. We will make a team, Toddy—the two of us there."

Tod laughed. "I'll come to your stall as soon as I finish the sweeping and cleaning, Mum. I must be off now." He waved and raced down a zigzag stairway.

Later that morning when Molly Tolliver appeared at her new stall at the zoo, she seemed to be refreshed. A bright blue ribbon sparkled around her thick, greying hair and she wore a starched white apron to cover the worn spots on her dress.

Mr Bartlett, in his tall silk hat and sharply pressed swallow-tail coat, happened to be passing by. He recognized Molly and tipped his hat.

"Welcome to the Gardens, Mrs Tolliver," he said.

Molly smiled back at him and watched him as he walked on. There was a whole new routine for her to learn. It would soon be Sunday afternoon, one of her favourite times, when the zoo was reserved just for the Fellows of the Gardens and their families and friends. The visitors today would be the privileged, the famous and the fashionable members of London society. Some of them would ride in elegant horse-drawn carriages around the Outer Circle. Special accommodations had been arranged for the servants to wait outside the Gardens at the entrance gate. Molly straightened herself in anticipation.

At this moment, Tod burst from the Elephant House, turning one perfect cartwheel after another as he headed towards his mother's stall. He was jubilant to have her nearby. She had promised to save the leftover buns for him, and he had promised himself that he would give half of them to Jumbo.

Tod made a low, sweeping circus bow to his mother and began to sing a popular song that all the sweepers and cleaners at the zoo often hummed.

> The O.K. thing to do on Sunday afternoon
> Is to toddle to the Zoo.
> Weekdays do for some, but not for me or
>   you.
> So dressed right, down the street, we show
>   them who is who.
> The walking in the Zoo, walking in the Zoo.
> The O.K. thing on Sundays is the walking
>   in the Zoo.

Molly laughed, then quickly grabbed Tod's arm and pulled him inside her stall. An elegant lady wearing a stiff green crinolined dress that belled out in back over a bustle was walking towards them. Her face was partly hidden by the wide brim of a feather-bedecked straw hat. She held the hand of a small boy who was immaculate in a white sailor suit.

"Oh Toddy, look at her beautiful dress," Molly sighed.

But Tod was more interested in watching Jumbo across the path. He was being led by Scotty through the iron-barred gate into the largest outdoor enclosure of the Elephant House. Scotty locked the gate firmly and then quickly freed the elephant.

Jumbo pawed the ground with his right front foot and then turned around and around, each time expanding his circle. He stopped abruptly. In front of him was a newly built large round pond.

Jumbo headed slowly for the pond and then stopped at the edge of it, pushing his left front foot cautiously along the shore. Was he testing the earth to see if it would bear the weight of a growing elephant? Was he remembering the slippery bank that had caused him to plunge into the turbulent river long ago in Africa?

He entered the water slowly. He squealed with joy and his huge cumbersome body fell like a rolling wave into the water. His trunk plunged downward and then sent up a spray of water as high as a fountain.

Jumbo tossed and turned and trumpeted until many of the Sunday afternoon visitors began to gather in large groups along the iron rail fence of his enclosure.

By this time most of Molly Tolliver's buns and apples had been bought by children as well as parents. Even Tod was among the onlookers holding out a smashed bun that his mother declared could not be sold.

Jumbo saw the gathering crowd and sniffed the food. He ambled from the pond, shaking beads of water into a blinding shower before walking to the fence.

Small hands lifted their treats as high as they could. Jumbo was pleased. He unfurled his trunk, twisted it up and over the fence and with magical speed twirled the treats into his mouth.

"Jumbo! Jumbo!" the children began to cry.

The lady in the green dress and the large straw hat appeared. Her small son held up his bun for the mammoth elephant.

"Oh, what a nasty-looking beast," the mother exclaimed when she caught sight of Jumbo.

"I think he's a love, Mother," the small boy piped up. "Look at his funny mouth."

Jumbo bent his head to peer more closely at the mother. Had he understood her? He swung his trunk above the fence, grabbed her straw hat and began stuffing it into his mouth. There was a noisy sound of crunching straw.

The children shrieked with laughter.

Scotty appeared at once from the Elephant House with a rope which he swung quickly over Jumbo's head.

He called to the distraught, angry mother. "Go to the superintendent's office for amends, madam. Please forgive Jumbo. This trick will not happen again."

Scotty scolded Jumbo and said in a stern voice, "No—No—No hats," as they left the outside enclosure. Scotty knew that his African elephant must continue to earn his reputation for good behaviour or he might not be allowed to remain in the zoo.

Tod raced back to the stand where he knew his mother was watching. They ducked their heads under the counter and laughed uproariously.

"Jumbo's revenge!" Molly cried.

6

For the rest of the day Jumbo was not allowed to go outside his room in the Elephant House. Scotty repeated the warning over and over—"No hats, no hats."

Jumbo spent his time butting his head into one of the walls and then hanging it like a repentant child and refusing to look at Scotty. He paced back and forth and stood by the hour in front of his door pawing it with his foot, which meant, "Open it!"

"I hope he's learned his lesson," Scotty said gruffly to Tod. Then he opened the door to the outside enclosure and Jumbo plunged into the fresh air. It was a bright sunny Monday when boys and girls spilled in overflowing numbers into the Zoological Gardens, for it was a six-pence day and the public was invited.

Jumbo headed for the fence where children with high-pitched voices cried, "Jumbo! Jumbo!" He shoved his trunk through the bars to be petted.

"The children love Jumbo," Tod confided to Scotty as they watched from the Elephant House. "I think they would like to get close to him without a fence in between."

"I have a plan up my sleeve that will do just that," Scotty said with a smug grin on his face. "But I'm not ready to announce it yet. Even you, Tod, will have to wait."

Tod knew better than to prod and beg. He wondered if Scotty would allow Jumbo to walk alone through the Gardens. Or would he let the children come into the Elephant House? He didn't have much time to think about it because Scotty had given him an important new job. Every noon when Scotty went for his midday meal, Tod was to stand outside Jumbo's fenced-in enclosure and report at once if anything went wrong.

"You're not to go inside with Jumbo when I'm not there," he warned Tod. "One trainer is enough for the elephant and that trainer is Matthew Scott."

"Scotty and Jumbo are like brothers," Tod confided later to his mother. "I doubt if one of them could get along without the other."

Guarding Jumbo's pen became the best time in Tod's day. Each noon he shared the stale buns from Molly's stand with Jumbo. He did his most difficult cartwheels in front of the amused eyes of his animal friend. He even began telling him secrets as he petted the elephant's long, wrinkled trunk.

"Someday," Tod whispered, "when Scotty gets too old to take care of you, then I will be your keeper. The next best thing to being a circus clown is to be an elephant trainer."

Tod was certain that Jumbo nodded his head at that.

Tod also shared his worries.

"My mum coughs all the time," he said sadly one day. "She even brings the black medicine bottle to her stall. If Mr Bartlett finds out she's sick he might take away her job."

Jumbo lowered his head and looked at Tod.

One noon when Tod was trying to stand on his head for Jumbo, his cap fell off. With the quickness of a snapping turtle, Jumbo grabbed it with his trunk. He waved it back and forth and stuck it on top of a fence post.

At this moment both Jumbo and Tod saw Scotty walking towards them. "No hats—no hats—no hats" resounded in their ears. Jumbo grabbed the cap and smashed it on top of Tod's head. They were silent when Scotty appeared. Jumbo blinked his eyes in innocence when his keeper walked up to him and announced that it would soon be time for Jumbo's daily hosing and scrubbing with the long-handled brush. Tod winked at the elephant and made a low, sweeping bow.

"So our young Tod thinks he's in the circus," Scotty said gruffly. Then he made a surprise announcement. Because of Jumbo's recent good behaviour, he told a gathering crowd of zoo workers, he was going to train him to take children for rides on his back.

Tod jumped into the air and for the first time in his life managed to twirl his body into a spin. Even Scotty was impressed.

"I might use you, Tod, to help with the training," he said.

Tod was ecstatic. In the circus, elephants took children for rides on their backs. It would be like living with the circus again.

The training started that afternoon after the crowds had left. Scotty produced a large wooden seat which he called a "howdah" and which had been built to fit Jumbo's back. He commanded several workers to climb up a small platform near the elephant and fasten the seat tightly with bands under Jumbo's stomach.

"Six children can ride at one time," Scotty explained. "Three will sit on each side, with their backs to the elephant and their knees facing outward. I'll strap them in tight so there will be no fallin' off."

He turned to Tod. "Now hop up and we'll give it a try."

"Kneel," Scotty commanded Jumbo. He had trained the elephant to bend his right knee at this command so he could step on his leg and climb up to scrub his ears and his fast-growing tusks.

"Kneel," he ordered again. Jumbo bent his knee and Tod leaped up and climbed into the howdah. He fastened the leather strap carefully over his lap.

Scotty took his position beside Jumbo's left front leg. He carried a bull-hook in one hand and the neck rope in the other and led Tod and Jumbo slowly along the path near Molly Tolliver's stand.

Jumbo appeared to be proud of the howdah and Tod on his back. He lifted his head and walked with longer strides than usual. But Molly ran outside her stall in alarm.

"Toddy!" she cried.

"Be calm, Mrs Tolliver," Scotty said softly. "Elephants can be frightened by unusual sounds or excitement."

Tod looked at his mother with a half-scared, half-elated grin. As he did so, a scuffling noise came from the house of Obaysch, the hippopotamus who lived around the corner from Molly's stall. The huge beast had come to the zoo several years before from the island of Obaysch on the White Nile. He seemed to have developed a strange liking for Turner. Turner and Obaysch's Arab keeper never left his side. The hippo was a prized possession of the Zoological Gardens and sometimes competed with Jumbo for attention.

Scotty disliked Obaysch and the hippo in turn disliked Scotty. The hippo lunged at him whenever Scotty came near his enclosure.

"That ugly beast with those gapin' jaws and those iceberg-lookin' teeth should be shipped back to the Nile," Scotty said loudly each time he passed the Hippopotamus House.

The scuffling noise grew louder and Jumbo became skittish. Scotty tightened his hold on the rope around Jumbo's neck and began leading him back to the Elephant House. Another keeper raced around the corner and rushed towards him.

"Mr Scott, Obaysch got loose!"

Scotty motioned for him to be quiet and pointed to Tod on Jumbo's back.

Jumbo began to snort nervously. Tod could feel the elephant's body tremble under the wooden seat.

Scotty grabbed the excited keeper and drew him near. He whispered as he steadily moved Jumbo towards his quarters.

"Don't get the elephant excited," he mumbled. "He could race after that fool hippo and flip the boy right off his back."

"Do you know what happened?" The keeper tried to keep his voice down. "That brute Obaysch pushed back the door of his den when the Arab sent for the carpenter to mend it. Mr Bartlett needs your help. He said that you should come at once!"

They were now near Jumbo's door. Scotty carefully opened it and led the elephant inside. Tod didn't have to be told to unfasten his leather strap and slide down Jumbo's back. He had heard the news about the hippo.

"Quick, Tod," Scotty said, "open a bag of hay for Jumbo. Stay with him until I get back. If he gets restless, give him some apples."

Tod couldn't believe his good luck. Scotty was allowing him to be in the paddock alone with Jumbo.

Scotty turned to Jumbo. "Good lad, good boy. You're going to be the best riding elephant in England."

Then he slid out the door with the keeper. Sure enough, they saw Obaysch waddling up the lane in front of them, squashing into mush a newly planted rose garden.

Mr Bartlett walked rapidly towards Scotty. "Scott." His voice was shaky. He found it difficult to control his emotions. "You know how Obaysch lunges at you whenever he catches you walking near him." Mr Bartlett paused to gasp for air. "Go in front of him and shout his name. I know he'll start after you." Mr Bartlett took another deep breath before continuing.

"Race into his house. There's a platform inside. Jump up on it. Then you can dash out over the fence. We'll be right behind you and bang the door down behind the charging beast."

Tod watched through a slit in Jumbo's door. To his amazement Jumbo nudged his head close beside him. He snorted with seeming delight at the sight of Obaysch outside his pen.

"Ugly brute! Ugly brute!" Scotty screamed. Obaysch turned his bulging eyes in Scott's direction. He lowered his head and charged, his short legs gathering the speed of a locomotive at full steam.

"Hurry, Scotty," Tod muttered under his breath. He clenched his fingers around the iron bar across Jumbo's door. Jumbo banged his foot on the floor. The hippo's fat belly appeared to skid along the ground, sending stones and sticks and plants in all directions.

Scotty bounded through the hippo's door with Obaysch almost at his heels. There was a clang as the door banged shut, and within minutes Scotty was climbing over the fence to safety and Obaysch was locked behind bars.

Tod grabbed Jumbo's trunk and swung it back and forth with joy.

Jumbo trumpeted, and Tod was certain that he was saying, "Victory."

7

Jumbo was blissfully content. He made soft squeals and trumpets each morning after breakfast when Scotty fastened the howdah on his back. Then he strode to his door and pawed at it impatiently. He wanted it to open, for he could hear the laughter of the children waiting for him outside.

They held out buns and Jumbo appeared to smack his lips as he stuffed one after another into his mouth. Scotty was surprised that there were no ill effects at all from so many treats. Jumbo's constant eating only seemed to make him grow.

Mr Bartlett walked by to observe "the elephant rides" and exclaimed with astonishment.

"Jumbo is still growing!"

Children lined up daily to climb onto this "moving mountain of an elephant" and feel the jolts and rhythms of real joints and legs carrying them high in the air above everyone else in the Gardens. They had a special look on their faces

53

as though they were doing something brave and risky, especially when they heard Scotty call out, "Step aside for the elephant with the children on his back, ladies and gentlemen. His swinging trunk could knock yer 'eads off."

Word of Scotty's brave run to capture the hippo had spread to every corner of the zoo. The children felt proud, too, to have him as their escort.

The newspapers of London printed stories about Jumbo's rides. The headlines read,

THE STAR OF THE LONDON ZOO
IS JUMBO.
HUNDREDS OF CHILDREN RIDE
ON JUMBO'S BACK IN ABSOLUTE
SAFETY.
QUEEN VICTORIA ANNOUNCES
THAT THE ROYAL CHILDREN WILL
BE GIVEN A RIDE ON JUMBO'S
BACK.

Scotty had never been so pleased with himself and Jumbo. He wore red buttons on his pepper-and-salt jacket and he polished his shoes. His moustache twisted in perfect rings on either side of his nose. His pockets jingled with the coins which children handed to Jumbo at the end of their rides and which the elephant promptly dropped into his keeper's pocket.

Jumbo received special treatment now. The solid brick Elephant House was scrubbed and polished and the carved elephant heads over all the entrances were washed and cared for as though they were real. Scotty was given living quarters on the upper floor of the house so he could keep constant watch over Jumbo, "the star of the zoo."

Tod was part of the excitement too, for Scotty often had him ride in the howdah to calm the more excited and nervous children. He bought him new knickers and two new shirts to mark the occasion of his first ride in public.

"Wot would all the fine folk think seein' a ragged boy on Jumbo's back?" Scotty explained.

Tod and his mother handled the new clothes with special care.

"Life is looking better for us, Toddy," Molly said one evening as the two of them sat at the table in their dimly lit room. Noises of hawking pedlars, wailing children and scuffling neighbours poured through their open window from the street below. They had been reading from an open school-book in front of them; Molly gave Tod lessons each evening when he returned from the zoo. Molly coughed and leaned her head against the wall behind her.

"The learning I have passed on to you, Toddy, is far more valuable than a bag full of coins," Molly sighed and wiped her eyes. "And your father, bless his soul, was the kindest of men. He taught you the beginnings of a fine career. A clown gives laughter to men and women and children. There is no better gift."

Tod interrupted. "What if someday I become the keeper of Jumbo?"

"That's something like being in a circus, Toddy, isn't it?" She kissed him lightly on the cheek, then went to her bed and was soon asleep.

But the happiness that burned like a bright light between Molly and Tod dimmed quickly the next morning. Molly was too ill to go to work.

"Tell Mr Bartlett that I will come tomorrow," she said to Tod as he got ready to leave.

He turned to her in surprise and dismay. He hadn't realized she was so ill. He quickly put a bun and a cup of steaming tea beside her bed. An uneasy fear twisted inside him and he thought he might also be sick. Mum did look bad. He could see the skeletal bones of her face in the grey morning light.

"I'll bring you apples and buns, Mum, and I'll come home early," said Tod, trying to sound cheerful.

"Toddy, sit down beside me for a minute before you go." Molly propped herself against her woollen shawl and gulped a large dose of black medicine.

"If I get too sick to work and the cough doesn't stop, I may have to go to the workhouse for a time."

"Oh Mum—not the workhouse!" Tears came to Tod's eyes. He thought he had buried forever the memory of the cuffings and drudgery and poor food during the month of their stay in one of the workhouses for the poor. It had happened just after his father had died and they had left the circus.

"It won't be long, Tod," she promised and then her face brightened.

"I've come upon a plan for you if my illness lasts longer than I expect. I've heard of a new program for poor children and orphans. They are going to be sent across the ocean to Canada to live and work on farms. It's a new kind of country, Toddy, where people are freer. It's a healthy, open place. . . ."

"But Mum, I'm not an orphan and I have a job and I won't leave you!" Tod cried loudly. He didn't care who might hear him.

"It's the best plan I can think of, son." Molly's eyes closed and she seemed to be drifting off to sleep. "We'll talk about it later. . . . Now go off to the zoo. . . . If I sleep a bit I'll feel better. . . ."

The morning outside was thick and heavy with fog. There were no helping hands or friendly smiles anywhere. Tod felt as lost and strange outside as he did inside himself. His thoughts raced ahead.

If his mother went to the workhouse he would have to go with her. But how could he be a cleaner and sweeper at the zoo? It was much too far to walk. And why did Mum want to send him across the ocean? He might never see her again. He might have to live on a farm in the new world. He could never be an elephant keeper or a clown.

Tod thought of his mother lying on the bed with her eyes closed, her skin stretched over her bones like pale transparent paper.

At the zoo, the buildings and the animals faded in and out of view in the fog and seemed to float like disembodied images through the dim and shifting greyness.

Tod felt a claw scrape over his shoulder.

Had the black bear escaped from his pit on the other side of the tunnel? Tod shivered. Last month, one of the bears had mauled a keeper to death and had to be shot. Tod froze for a frightening second and then swung his hand around and struck. The sharp object was only the branch of a tree.

Tod ran breathlessly to the Elephant House and jumped inside. It was warm, and filled Tod with a feeling of comfort. Scotty was scrubbing Jumbo's back with the long-handled brush, and the big elephant reached out to Tod with his trunk and stroked his back.

"Well Tod," said Scotty, without turning his head, "Molly can stay at home today. There won't be a single customer. Even the rats will stay in their bloomin' holes on a day like this."

"I'm sure she won't come," Tod replied. "She's sick." He didn't dare say more to Scotty

about his mother and what she had said to him
about going to Canada.

He waited until Scotty released Jumbo into
his outdoor enclosure and left for his midday
lunch. Then he quickly ran to his mother's stall
for the bag of leftover buns. He ate a few of
them hungrily, put aside the best ones for Molly
and took the others to Jumbo's pen.

Jumbo trumpeted cheerfully when he saw
Tod coming. He was in a playful mood, and as
he stuffed the buns into his mouth, he began
crazily swaying from foot to foot. Then he
pushed his trunk between the fence bars to be
petted.

Tod put his arms around the elephant's trunk
and began to cry. The account of his mother's
cough and her death-like face and her plan to
send him across the ocean poured over the elephant's sensitive trunk and into his flapping
ears. He stood patiently and listened.

Tod's burdens lightened. He went about his
tasks with his mops and brooms for the remain-
der of the foggy day and even laughed with
some of the other young sweepers and cleaners
as they hid from each other in the shifting
earth-bound fog.

At the end of the day Tod grabbed the buns
and an apple from Jumbo's lunch and raced
across the Gardens towards home. He felt light-
hearted. His mother would be better, he was
certain, and they would sit over the school-books

and read the history of England and do his sums.

As he entered the creaking tenement building and started to climb up the stairs, he was stopped by the stout, dishevelled man who collected their monthly rent.

"I have bad news for you, lad," he barked as though issuing a command. "Your mother was deathly ill this afternoon. When we heard her cries, we tried to help, but the people from the workhouse had to come for her."

Tod's heart began to beat so loudly that he could hardly hear. His mouth felt dry as though dust were blowing in and out of it and leaving no room at all for words.

The man's voice pounded on. "Don't worry, lad. The workhouse folks said you could come to them in the morning. There was no time for them to find you at the zoo. Your mum needed a doctor at once."

Tod shivered. The stout man noticed, and softened his voice.

"Why don't you keep your sweeping job at the zoo?" he asked. "The people there are fair-minded folks. They will find you a room."

Tod started to leave. The man's voice stabbed at him again.

"You'll have to be out tomorrow, Tod Tolliver," he said. "Your room is already rented to someone else."

He held out a pudgy hand. Tod backed away

from it as though it were responsible for this terrible happening. He tore up the stairs and threw open the door. Molly was not there. Even her bed was gone, as well as all the chairs. In the centre of what had been their home was the rickety table and on top of it were his possessions—two school-books, the new pants and shirts that Scotty had bought for him, an extra pair of socks and his mother's woollen shawl. Beside the table was the narrow cot that had been his bed.

Tod grabbed one of the school-books to leaf inside for something that had always been there. It lay between the pages of the lesson he and Mum had worked on just last night. It was a picture of his mother and father under a circus tent, and peeping out between them was Tod, aged four. Tod held it in his shaking hand and then carefully slid the photograph into the pocket of the shirt that he was wearing.

Tod suddenly hated this room without his mother in it. He wanted to break the windows and kick the table into a million splinters. Why didn't the workhouse people wait for him? His mother needed him. He could help her. He wanted to be with her. The wooden boards beneath the window of his room began to creak.

Tod became frantic. The booming voice downstairs had said that the workhouse people were expecting him tomorrow. He dreaded going there again but he couldn't stay here another minute. He began piling his books and clothes into his mother's shawl. He threw the bundle over his shoulder and walked silently down the stairs.

Outside on the street, sheets of fog wrapped around him and this time he was grateful that he couldn't be seen. He began to walk to the only other place that seemed like home—the London Zoological Gardens. It was dark when he finally got there and he had to crawl under the great front gate which was already locked for the night. He didn't want to go to the Elephant House and wake Scotty and Jumbo.

Tod looked down the path in front of him and saw the tunnel. He would seek shelter there from the night and watch the great clock on the top of the Lion House nearby. No one would bother him in the zoo at night.

Tod crept into the dark passage and wrapped his mother's shawl around him. It felt warm and comforting. He pressed his face into one of its folds and began to sob bitterly until at last he fell asleep.

When Tod woke in the morning, it was six o'clock on the round, steady clock. The fog had settled into a misty drizzle. He felt the warmth of his mother's wool shawl and then remembered with sudden horror the day before.

Tod could hear the lions roar from their house beneath the clock. He could see the sweepers and cleaners hurrying down the path nearby with their banging buckets and brushes. Soon one of them would walk through the tunnel. He grabbed his possessions and wrapped them quickly inside the shawl, then tucked them behind some bushes.

He began walking toward the Elephant House. He knew he would have to tell Scotty at once about his mother and he also knew that he had to stay with Jumbo. He would beg Scotty to find a room nearby where he could live until his mother was well again. Tomorrow he would go to see her at the workhouse.

But when Tod arrived at the Elephant House there was turmoil. Jumbo was pacing back and forth behind his outdoor iron fence, trumpeting for attention.

Inside the house, Tod could hear elephant squeals and moans. Scotty's raspy voice shouted, "Tod!" Bring clean rags and buckets of water! Clumsy Alice has ripped off the end of her trunk!"

Tod hurried inside. Alice was suffering. Tiny whimpers came from her open mouth. Scotty held the bandaged trunk that hung as lifeless as a dead reptile. To lift it brought only pain to the elephant.

"She ripped the trunk on a jagged stone," Scotty tried to explain. "Dip water into her mouth, Tod," he ordered. "We'll have to feed her day and night until she's healed."

Other helpers began to arrive. Superintendent Bartlett was called. He talked to Scotty and together they ordered fresh bandages and healing ointment and a crew of animal keepers to feed poor Alice until the damaged trunk was healed.

Tod was assigned to spread fresh hay, apples and carrots in Jumbo's paddock. He hastily ate some of the bread and an apple and washed himself in the fresh pail of water. Jumbo smelled the food and marched inside. He paid no attention to the cries of Alice.

Scotty now had a strict rule that no one could be alone in the room with Jumbo but himself and Mr Bartlett. But Tod could talk and pet his friend through the bars on the inside door.

Tod reached for Jumbo's trunk and at once poured out the whole story of his mother's illness into Jumbo's ears. He even told him about sleeping in the tunnel and about the plan to send him across the ocean.

"I can't go off to Canada and leave Mum and you and Scotty," said Tod as he held Jumbo's trunk more tightly. "I have to help my mum. . . . I'll have to eat some of your food, Jumbo, to keep from starving."

8

Alice was the centre of everyone's attention at the Elephant House on the day of her injury, and there wasn't a second when Tod could talk with Scotty or Mr Bartlett alone. They didn't even notice that Molly hadn't arrived at her stall, for splashing rain fell from the sky and kept all visitors away.

Tod fed and watered Jumbo and let him outside in the rain while he cleaned his stall. He was sent running for more bandages and clean buckets of water for Alice. The day ended early and the sky became black and foreboding. Tod couldn't walk to the workhouse now. He would never be able to find it in the dark. There was no answer but for him to return to the black, lonely tunnel for the night. He dreaded going. The night before, he had heard rats scratching along the tunnel paths and he had listened to the wild night cries of the lions and the bears nearby. He had felt as if his whole body was being squeezed by a tightly drawn rope.

But he finally hurried to the tunnel to get out of the rain and was relieved to find his bundle where he had left it. He grabbed his mother's shawl and hugged it tightly around him.

The wind turned biting cold and swept straight through the long hole of his makeshift bedroom. The shawl was no protection, and in the morning Tod woke early with a stabbing headache and a cough that sounded like his mother's.

He gathered his bundle and ran at once to the Elephant House and stood before Scotty—dirty, dishevelled and sniffling. His story of Molly, the workhouse, the tunnel and all his misery were laid out in vivid detail before Scotty.

Scotty looked at Tod as though appraising him for the first time and said calmly, "It just happens that my old Aunt Stubbs has a dry space in her attic. And she's lookin' for a boy to do her chores for the use of it. I'll see her at noon and tell her about you."

"But I can't give up my job at the zoo!" Tod was alarmed.

"Who said you had to give it up?" Scotty was blunt. "A lad like you can do both jobs."

Scotty scratched an address on a bit of torn newspaper.

"I'll go tonight," Tod answered eagerly. He felt such a flood of relief that he wanted to whirl into a dozen cartwheels. Instead he coughed and wiped his nose on the sleeve of his shirt.

"And Tod," Scotty turned away from him and began brushing Jumbo's back. "You better go see your mum tomorrow. You can take the day off."

Tod was amazed by these generous offers from rough-talking Scotty. He had a sudden impulse to throw his arms around this keeper whom the zoo people agreed was "as cold as a frozen mackerel towards people" and "as gentle as a mother hen towards most of the animals." Obaysch the hippo was the one exception.

All Tod managed to say was, "Thank you, Mr Scott."

"Now get along with you. I've work to do." Scotty shoved Tod away with an impatient wave of his hand.

All day, as Tod scrubbed and washed animal cages, he felt relief about the "dry space" where he would sleep. He also helped with Alice, who still needed constant attention. Everyone was assured that she would recover and be able to use her ragged trunk again.

Tod worried about the trip to the workhouse. It would take him hours to walk there. He wondered if anyone would recognize him from the miserable month that he and Molly had lived there. Surely his mother would be better after two days of rest and care.

At the end of his sweeping and cleaning day, Tod was exhausted and sick. He scooped up his few possessions in his mother's shawl and headed for a dingy street not too far from the tenement where he had lived with his mother.

Scotty's scrap of paper directed him to an even more crowded part of the city. The streets were narrow and wretched. Mud stuck to his shoes and the air was full of vile odours. Tod came to a little row of scruffy houses with small peaked roofs that were patched and rotting. On one of them he saw the number on Scotty's paper. A drunken man loitered around the door, but Tod was used to such people and slid quickly around him. He banged on the door because it lacked both bell-handle and knocker.

The door creaked open, and from behind it peered the most crinkly-skinned old woman Tod had ever seen. He couldn't tell if her eyes were open or closed. Thin, white wisps of hair hung like strands of thread below an ancient dust cap. She had difficulty lifting her head above the rounded hump of her back.

"Scotty's boy?" she rasped.

Tod nodded.

A dim lamp burned above a small table, revealing a tidy but barren room. The old woman handed Tod a lighted candle, stuck into a ginger bottle, which gave an even feebler light.

"Up to the attic," she ordered, pointing to a tiny stairway. "I'll rap for you in the morning to do the chores."

She waved Tod off with a fast sweep of her crooked cane.

There was no doubt in Tod's mind that Aunt Stubbs and Scotty were related. They both seemed unable to be openly friendly.

At the top of the stairs, Tod flashed the candle about to survey the "dry space." It was too low for standing and too narrow to be a real room, but there was a mattress on the floor with a heavy woollen blanket on top of it. It was pushed into a corner beneath the sloping roof where it was sheltered and dry. Beside the mattress stood a weathered chest of drawers with a space on top for his books. Tod unpacked them at once and put his mother's shawl and his clothes in the chest. Then he took the photo of his mother, father and himself under the circus tent and propped it against the books.

The small space curled around Tod like a comfortable nest. He had a home again and he felt an urgent need to thank someone. Scotty wasn't there. He would tell the ancient woman in the morning how he felt, but for now he bowed his head and said a prayer that Molly had taught him. He slipped off his pants and shirt, crawled under the blanket and fell asleep at once.

A loud rap on the floor woke Tod early in the morning. He looked up expecting to see the time on the round clock above the Lion House of the zoo. But there were only thin shafts of light peeping through the half-rotted roof above his head. He remembered Aunt Stubbs and her tiny room. He slipped on his clothes and raced down the narrow stairs. He was over-flowing with good thoughts about the old woman. She met him with her cane, pointing to the table and a steaming bowl of porridge. Tod was overwhelmed. He hadn't had a hot morsel inside him since the day his mother went away.

"Thank you, thank you," he said, hurrying to the table.

"Don't whisper at me, boy," the old woman shrieked in a high monotone. "I can hardly hear a word you say."

The chores for Aunt Stubbs were not easy. Tod scrubbed and swept. He carried water and wood into the house and he nailed down some loose boards in the floor. Not a smile or a word passed between him and the old woman. Tod decided that she was like her nephew—quiet and sullen with people. At last she pounded her cane on the floor and said, "Now you can go."

Tod raced out the door. He had no difficulty finding his way to the workhouse through the narrow streets. He remembered each turn, and here and there recognized a squalid shop where he and Molly had sometimes bought things when they had any money. He avoided the tene-ment building that had been their home, and when he came near it he pulled his cap far down so no one would know him.

The trip to the workhouse seemed endless, but when Tod came near the familiar desolate building he began to shiver as though a shower of icicles was piercing his body. The starvation and thrashings he remembered at the work-house were as fresh in his mind as though they had happened yesterday.

But Tod was determined to keep his thoughts on his mother. He straightened his shoulders and started to lift the latch on the iron gate, when a ragged boy struggling with a bucket of slop brushed against him.

There was instant recognition. The two of them had shared the same rough, hard bed in the sleeping ward, and once they had spent a night together in a cold cellar as punishment.

"Tod!"

"Colin!" They exclaimed in unison.

The bucket was pushed behind some tangled shrubs and the two of them squeezed behind it.

Tod listened eagerly as his thin, pale friend told about Molly Tolliver coming to the work-house and about the parish doctor saying that her illness was contagious, and how the doctor made them move her thirty miles away into another workhouse where no one would be allowed to visit.

"Did she ask for me? Did she speak my name?" Tod was desperate.

"I heard her," Colin confided. "She said to the doctor . . . 'See that my boy is safe. He

works as a sweeper in the Zoological Gardens.'
Then she said, 'If I don't recover, I want him to
go to a farm in Canada.'"

A man's snarling voice interrupted them.

"Get out of them bushes, Colin . . . and
who's the sneakin' lad with you?"

A strong hand grabbed Tod's shoulder. Tod
twisted away. He did a springing jump and a
high cartwheel and sped away down the narrow,
dirty street without turning his head or pausing
for a full breath of air. He ran until he couldn't
breathe at all and found himself beside an
empty shop front where he lay exhausted until
it was dark. He didn't want to be taken to the
workhouse as a runaway.

Tod was heartsick about his mother. He could
not visit her now that she was in a special ward.
What was her terrible illness, he wondered?
And why was she so determined that he should
go across the ocean? He got up wearily to go to
his new home.

The door was opened by the old woman, as it
had been the night before. This time she
peered at him with half-opened eyes that
seemed to express some interest in what she
saw.

"A dirty boy," she cried, and pointed with her
cane to a basin of water. Beside it on the table
Tod saw a bowl of stew. It smelled delicious.

Like a crouching toad, Aunt Stubbs stood
over Tod until he finished both washing and

then eating, and without a word pointed upward with her cane.

She can't hear one word I say, Tod thought, so I'll thank her with a circus stunt. He twirled about on one foot, spun into a ball, then slowly unfolded into his normal self.

When he finished, the hunched old woman smiled and her face looked almost friendly. Tod went up to bed thinking that, if nothing else, he was safe at Aunt Stubbs's.

9

The rough, cold, windy days of winter arrived and Tod shivered through his morning chores until Aunt Stubbs produced an ancient fur-lined coat that was wonderfully warm and felt as snug as though he had just crawled into a rabbit hole.

Tod worried constantly about his mother and her illness. Both Scotty and Mr Bartlett sent letters to the workhouse about Molly and found that her illness might be consumption, the plague of the poor. They wrote assuring her that Tod would have a steady job at the zoo and a warm room where he could live.

Molly wrote back to Tod immediately. Her words drifted in weak feathery lines over the page.

Toddy,

I am very ill, but it is a comfort to know that you are at the zoo and that

you have a warm place to live. Bless Mr
Bartlett and Mr Scott. Now I can forget
about sending you abroad. Write to
me. My love to you.

Mother

Tod at once wrote an answer—telling his
mother about Alice and his warm, dry room.
He even described the bowls of hot porridge
and the delicious stews. He began writing to her
every week.

But there were long lapses between Molly's
replies and sometimes she wrote only, "I love
you, Toddy."

The raw, icy weather continued. Visitors were
scarce and both Jumbo and Scotty became irri-
table and restless.

The elephant was still growing, and his
appetite seemed to be increasing. The fresh buns
and fruit from all the children who piled onto his
back for rides, plus the bags of hay, oats and
beans, the buckets of carrots, potatoes, cabbages
and onions and the loaves of bread didn't seem
to fill him up. Jumbo could no longer squeeze
through the zoo's eleven-foot-high tunnel.

"He's over eleven feet tall and he weighs
almost seven tons!" Scotty shook his head with
amazement when Jumbo's latest measurements
were announced.

"He must be the largest elephant in the
whole world!" Tod exclaimed. He looked at his

huge friend with admiration.

One night Jumbo banged against the side of the Elephant House and drove his tusks into the iron plates on the door of his paddock. Both tusks were broken at the ends.

Tod was alarmed. "Is he growing too big for the Elephant House?" he asked Scotty.

Jumbo's keeper was grim and silent.

Because of Jumbo's broken tusks, sores developed below both of his eyes. They became bloodshot with pain. Jumbo's restless feet padded back and forth in his small enclosure. He bellowed and the sound was like the shrill, urgent tone of a trumpet sounding an alarm.

Mr Bartlett came at once.

"We must cut through the skin and discharge the poison from the sores immediately," the superintendent said. Scotty agreed and Tod was called to guard the door and not allow anyone to enter.

A long steel rod with a sharp hook at the end was carefully put together by Mr Bartlett. Scotty stood beside Jumbo, calming him with soothing words.

"We're going to help you, Jumbo. . . . Good Jumbo."

Mr Bartlett stood under the elephant's lower jaw and moved the long instrument over one of the sores. Then he quickly cut through the skin.

Jumbo shrieked, and Tod quickly opened the door a crack to see what was happening. He was

certain that Jumbo's grey, crinkled skin had
turned blue. But Jumbo showed relief, even
though his great body trembled. The poison
began to drain from his cheek.

Within a short time, the second abscess was
opened. Jumbo slumped against a wall and
lifted his trunk feebly for Scotty to clean it. Tod
was called to bring fresh pails of water.

The abscesses healed and his tusks continued
to grow, but Jumbo was still restless and irrita-
ble. One night he smashed the doors of his
room. Massive timbers had to be hauled in by
workmen to reinforce the building. Mr Bartlett
and the distinguished Fellows of the zoo began
to worry. Some of them felt that the elephant
was big enough and strong enough to break
down almost any barrier. He might do terrible
damage.

Tod was now forbidden to go inside the
Elephant House when Jumbo was there. But he
refused to believe that his best friend had
become dangerous. Each day at noon, he
pressed his mouth against Jumbo's door and
talked to him. He could hear the elephant's
trunk brushing back and forth on the other
side.

He hears me, Tod thought and was comforted a little.

Scotty was the only person allowed to enter
Jumbo's quarters. All rides on the great elephant's back were cancelled. Massive, gentle,

fun-loving Jumbo became a stranger to many who had known him. Only at night, after the gates of the zoo were locked and Scotty took him for long walks through the gardens, did he become gentle and quiet.

"What's happened to Jumbo?" everyone asked.

"Has he grown too large for the zoo?"

"Is he yearning for Africa?"

"Is the Elephant House too small for him?"

Mr Bartlett tried to give an answer. "It may be a time of bad temper called *musth* that grown male elephants have for several weeks each year," he said. "If this is the problem, Jumbo must be kept in isolation and guarded until it goes away."

Scotty talked with no one, and buried his chin inside the collar of his new coat, hunching his shoulders and walking about with dragging steps.

Tod was bewildered. He wanted to help his friend. He wanted to stroke his trunk and feed him. He wrote to his mother about him. She loved Jumbo too. He yearned to talk with her but visits were still forbidden. Mr Bartlett planned to visit the workhouse where Molly was being treated. He might move her to another place, he told Scotty.

But the superintendent's immediate worry was Jumbo. Each day now at the Zoological Gardens there were shaking heads and spreading rumours about Jumbo. A report came from the Fellows after an emergency meeting that it was not possible to keep an animal in the zoo if it threatened to destroy its quarters and might become a danger to the public. Jumbo might have to go. But where?

Scotty held his hands over his ears when this report reached the Elephant House. Tod squeezed his eyes shut to keep the tears from falling down his cheeks.

"Jumbo will get well again, won't he, Scotty?" Tod confronted the silent keeper. "The problem of *musth* with grown-up elephants just lasts three weeks each year. That isn't very long."

Scotty didn't answer, he just shrugged.

And Jumbo did appear to get better. Scotty cautiously allowed him to enter his outdoor enclosure and to accept buns and fruit through the strong iron fence from the throngs of children. But the rides on his back were still cancelled.

"Jumbo is well and he is still growing!" Tod shouted to Aunt Stubbs over his nightly bowl of hot stew.

"What did you say, boy?" she cupped her ear.

Tod did three flips and a jump to make her smile.

But the soft days that appeared to glow with bright sunshine over Jumbo's improvement faded quickly into another winter storm, and its effects crept into the Elephant House with an uneasy chill.

When Tod entered the House one windy morning to sweep and clean Jumbo's paddock, he found Scotty slumped almost lifeless on his bench, patting Jumbo's head. The elephant playfully reached into his pocket and pulled out his handkerchief. Scotty lifted his head as Tod came in. His face was ghostly white and his eyes were red-rimmed and puffy.

"They're selling Jumbo," he muttered in a hollow, ringing voice. "He's going to America."

"No! It can't be true!" Tod shouted. "Somebody told you a lie."

"Then go to Mr Bartlett's office and ask." Scotty leaned his head against Jumbo's trunk.

Tod raced from the Elephant House to Mr Bartlett's office. A crowd of sweepers and cleaners and keepers of animals was gathered around the door. An assistant stood in front of them.

"The story is true," he answered Tod's question soberly. "If Jumbo were to have a dreadful rampage during one of his periods of *musth*, people might be killed. And he has grown too large for his quarters."

"Who is buying him?" Tod asked shakily. His voice was out of control.

"He has been sold to Phineas T. Barnum, the great American showman, for his circus. The circus has large facilities to care for Jumbo during his times of bad temper. He will have a more active life there than we can provide for him here."

"Barnum—the circus!" Tod shouted again. He was stunned by the news. Barnum was a man his father had admired. His circus was called "The Greatest Show on Earth." He should feel proud and excited that Jumbo was going to join it. Yet, how could he part with his best friend? Scotty and Jumbo could never be separated. What would the hundreds of children do when they came to Jumbo's outdoor enclosure and found him gone? Tod's thoughts were in turmoil.

The story of Jumbo's sale passed from mouth to mouth among the busy staff of the Zoological Gardens. They expressed shock and dismay, but among some of the Fellows there was relief that the problem of housing the "largest elephant in captivity," who was still growing, had been solved.

Scotty refused to talk. His lips became a thin line across his face, as if they were clamped together with a lock. He opened them only when he and Jumbo walked close together each evening through the deserted Gardens.

Tod talked endlessly to Jumbo, trying to explain the sale and what might happen to him. But Jumbo had become his playful, friendly self again. He swept Tod's cap off his head and waved it back and forth in the breeze before plunking it back in its proper place.

"Jumbo, you must be serious," Tod cried out at him in frustration. "You're going across the ocean. I might never see you again."

The sale of Jumbo was not widely known until January 25, 1882, when *The Times* of London published a story under the heading THE GREAT AFRICAN ELEPHANT. It read:

> Barnum, the American showman, has bought for the sum of £2000, the large male African Elephant which has for many years formed one of the principal attractions in the gardens of the Zoological Society in the Regent's-park.

Tod read the story aloud to Scotty and other keepers at the zoo.

Scotty shook his head.

"Mr Bartlett will change his mind," Tod tried to speak with confidence. "He loves Jumbo as much as we do."

But both Scotty and Tod abruptly faced reality on a cold, drizzly day when Barnum's men arrived at the zoo with a giant-sized crate. Jumbo was to be hauled in it to the London docks and placed on board the *Persian Monarch*, due to sail for the United States the following Sunday!

Tod grabbed some bars at the back of the crate and shook them violently in his rage.

When news of the crate's arrival appeared in several newspapers, readers all over England suddenly became outraged.

The editor of the *Daily Telegraph* sent Barnum a wire which he printed in his paper.

> All British children distressed at elephant's departure. Hundreds of correspondents beg us to enquire on what terms you will kindly return Jumbo.

Barnum replied immediately. His cable was printed on the front pages of all the leading newspapers.

> Fifty-one millions of American citizens anxiously awaiting Jumbo's arrival. . . . Jumbo's presence here imperative. Hundred thousand pounds would be no inducement to cancel purchase.

To Scotty, Tod and Jumbo's other friends at the zoo, the message was like a death warrant. Hundreds of visitors began arriving at the zoo. They wanted to see their beloved Jumbo before he was carted off to America in the ominous crate with its strong pitch-pine planking bound together by massive iron straps.

"There's only a small gap at the top for his trunk to stick through," Tod protested helplessly. "Jumbo can barely see outside."

10

Worry and uncertainty hung like heavy clouds over the Zoological Gardens, pressing down on everyone except Jumbo. He enjoyed the swelling crowds and their armloads of buns and cakes.

The sale of the great elephant had been declared official and Jumbo was passed into the hands of his American owners. Scotty took the news with sealed lips, but for some unknown reason there was no longer a slumping hopelessness in his manner. Tod was surprised.

It was now the job of "Elephant Bill" Newman of the Barnum Circus to get Jumbo out of the Gardens and onto the waiting ship. Mr Bartlett and Scotty had no idea how this would be done. Tod, pretending to be busy with his cleaning brushes, listened intently.

The three of them watched as Mr Newman approached Jumbo. The new keeper began dragging heavy chains over the floor and attaching them to Jumbo's front feet. He asked Scotty to help.

Jumbo became angry. He must have wondered why Scotty would allow this strange man to treat him like this. He pulled and jerked his legs, lifting the chains in his trunk and throwing them onto the floor as if he were trying to break them. Scotty calmed Jumbo by whispering into his flapping ear.

Mr Newman was impatient. He had deadlines to meet. The ship was waiting. He ordered more chains to be run over Jumbo's head, around his body and between his legs.

"The chains will be fastened inside the crate so Jumbo will be held firmly in place for the lifting and the moving," Mr Newman explained to Mr Bartlett and Scotty.

Now Jumbo was frightened, and Scotty's whispering reassurances no longer helped. He plunged from side to side and bellowed. But Mr Newman persisted and led Jumbo in chains up a ramp to the entrance of the crate.

Jumbo sensed danger ahead. He shook his massive head and suddenly lay down flat on his stomach with his hind legs stretched out behind him. His chains scattered like tangled ribbons.

"Hurrah, Jumbo!" Tod called.

Elephant Bill was embarrassed. He prodded and coaxed Jumbo. He offered him buns and fruit. Jumbo would not move. Mr Newman was not accustomed to disobedience from an elephant.

"We'll change our plans," he announced abruptly. "We'll walk this stubborn elephant the six miles to St Katharine's Docks early tomorrow morning. That should exhaust him and he'll be ready to enter the crate." He exuded confidence. "We'll board the ship on time and sail on the afternoon tide."

He ordered Scotty to take Jumbo back to his quarters. Scotty bent down and again whispered into Jumbo's ear. The elephant lifted himself slowly to his great height, and, turning around, followed his old keeper back into the Elephant House. Still in chains, Jumbo was a sad sight.

That night Scotty stayed by Jumbo's side. Tod huddled in a pile of straw in the storage room nearby, beside his pails and brushes.

Early the next morning Tod brought a farewell breakfast to his chained friend. He stroked the swinging trunk and choked back tears when he tried to say goodbye.

"I guess you can come along, Tod," Scotty said finally. "You can help with Jumbo until he boards the ship, then Barnum's men and boys take over." Scotty expressed no emotion and Tod was puzzled again. Wasn't it breaking his heart that Jumbo was leaving? Had he turned into a stone?

Scotty looped the rope around Jumbo's neck and led him slowly down the gravel path.

"He'll never walk down this path again, Mr Scott," Tod said softly. To himself he thought it seemed more like a funeral march than a daily stroll. Scotty said nothing.

Word had spread through the night and early hours of dawn on Sunday that there was trouble at the Zoological Gardens. Large crowds began to gather outside the entrance gate before daylight.

As Jumbo trudged through the gates in his clanking chains, he seemed surprised and then pleased by the group of cheering supporters.

"This is Jumbo's first time outside the Gardens since he came here as a young elephant," Scotty said quietly. Tod noticed that his eyes were misty.

"Does he have to go out in chains, Mr Scott?" Tod pleaded. The heavy chains seemed to add to his own burden of misery. "He looks like a prisoner."

Jumbo might have thought this too, for he angrily shook his chains, looked over the crowds and then calmly knelt down and rolled onto his side. He made no effort at all to get up and go any further.

Mr Newman was shocked and angry. He issued a brisk command. Jumbo answered by waving his trunk at the spectators. Elephant Bill cajoled and prodded again as he had done the day before. Tod thought he saw Jumbo look at Scotty and then trumpet slyly. The elephant answered Mr Newman this time by rolling on his back and kicking his feet in the air.

The crowds of people began to cheer. "Jumbo

doesn't want to leave his friends!" they shouted.

Jumbo turned back on his side and waved his trunk about pleasantly. There was no anger or fright in the gesture. He did, however, begin to trumpet loudly as though in answer to the cheering crowds.

There was an immediate response to the trumpets from the distant Elephant House. Alice began to whimper and moan and set off such a din that the other zoo animals were wakened. They added their growls and cries until the noise became a chorus of animal protests.

"It's Alice, Jumbo's wife," someone in the crowd cried out. "She's broken hearted that he's being taken away from her."

A smartly dressed man hustled through the crowd and ran to Mr Newman's side. They shook their heads and talked secretly by shielding their mouths with a newspaper. Then the gentleman turned back into the crowds and raced away.

It wasn't long until the secret was out. The gentleman was P.T. Barnum's London agent. He was sending a frantic cable to his boss in New York City.

> Jumbo has laid down in the street and won't get up. What shall we do?

Within hours another cable crossed the ocean from Barnum, the circus showman whom many called "the Prince of Humbugs and Master of Ballyhoo." It, too, became known to the public.

> Let Jumbo lie in the road for a week if
> he wants to. It is the best advertisement
> in the world.

Back at the entrance of the Zoological Gardens, Jumbo remained contentedly on the ground.

Mr Newman threw up his hands in defeat. "We can never get to the docks now in time for the sailing of the ship," he admitted. He motioned for Scotty to take charge of the enormous sprawling elephant.

Scotty merely pointed to the zoo and Jumbo struggled to a standing position. He shifted his chains into place and headed back into the Gardens.

A roar of approval rose from the swelling number of supporters and Tod's cries were among them. He leaped into the air like a bright, carefree balloon.

"If Jumbo won't leave his home in the Gardens," Tod called out to Scotty, "no one can force a seven-ton animal to move."

Stories of Jumbo's brave resistance to leaving his friends and home reached not only the people who flocked to the Zoological Gardens but also the newspapers in all parts of the English-speaking world.

As Jumbo plodded into the Elephant House,

shaking his chains, there was an outburst of
rejoicing. Alice did appear to be happy with
Jumbo's return. For the first time since she had
come to the zoo, she intertwined her healed but
oddly shaped trunk with Jumbo's when they
came close together. The public support for
Jumbo's effective and gentle refusal to leave the
Gardens grew like a rolling ball of snow.

A wreath of flowers, large enough to be hung
around Jumbo's neck, was delivered to the
Elephant House on the night of his return with
a note which read:

> A trophy of triumph over his brutal
> owners and American kidnappers.

Tod became the reader of newspaper stories
about Jumbo for Scotty and his fellow sweepers
and cleaners.

"Listen to this one," he laughed one morning, holding a newspaper in both hands.

> Jumbo said to Alice, "I love you."
> Alice said to Jumbo, "I don't believe
> you do.
> You wouldn't go to Yankeeland and
> leave me in the Zoo."

"And listen to this," Tod continued to read.
"'A young couple announces that they have
christened their newly arrived son 'Jumbo.'"

The sweepers and cleaners looked at Jumbo
and laughed until their sides ached.

The following day a copy of *Punch*, a popular
magazine, was brought to the Elephant House.
It contained a special poem.

As usual, Tod read it out loud, but this time
he swung one of his arms like a trunk.

> If *I* owned Jumbo
> (Who declines to go)
> Would I sell him to a Show?
> No, no, not I.
> When the Titan I saw
> Firmly planted his paw,
> I would shout 'HOORAW'
> For his bra-ve-ry.
>
> Chorus:
> If an army of Yankees should proffer their
> pay,
> I'd button my pockets, and send them away.
>
> What forget all the fun?
> All the tricks he has done?
> The ride and the bun?
> No, no, not I.

"It's Jumbomania," Scotty declared, pushing
back his bowler hat and swaggering with jaunty
steps through the zoo.

Not all the newspaper stories were clever

songs and poems. Important, serious-minded people in London became involved in the protest against Jumbo's sale. Questions were being asked in the House of Commons. The editor of *Vanity Fair*, a major publication, announced that he was starting a Jumbo Defence Fund. Queen Victoria and the Prince of Wales expressed their disapproval of the sale.

Attendance at the zoo rose daily. The gate-keeper announced that ticket sales were seven times larger than for the same days the year before. Paying visitors numbered in the thousands.

Jumbo was sublimely happy with the masses of visitors who crowded outside his fenced-in enclosure. His chains had been removed. Buns and fruit were thrown to him in unlimited numbers. His appetite was endless.

Buns even began to arrive by post. One day a gold neck chain and a loving cup were addressed "For Jumbo." Elephant Bill Newman and the Fellows of the Zoological Gardens became more and more embarrassed. Mr Newman, however, was a shrewd animal trainer with all the prestige of a circus man from "The Greatest Show on Earth." He refused to leave the Gardens, for P.T. Barnum had ordered him to stay.

One day when Scotty was at lunch, Tod overheard a conversation between Mr Newman and Superintendent Bartlett.

"Mr Scott and Jumbo have been together for many years. They know each other so well that even the smallest move of a finger or the wink of an eye could be a special order for the elephant."

"I wonder," Mr Bartlett stroked his beard, "if Scotty secretly passed along a message when Jumbo lay down on the road?"

Newman nodded.

Such a thing could have happened, Tod had to admit to himself. He was secretly happy that Scotty had been so clever.

The next morning there was a shocking announcement at the Elephant House. Matthew Scott had been offered a job with P.T. Barnum and would accompany Jumbo to America. He would become Jumbo's keeper in the Barnum circus.

The news hit Tod like an explosion. All his hopes that Jumbo might stay in the Garden were shattered as though they had been consumed by fire. Now Jumbo would co-operate with Scotty and walk into his crate. Both of them would leave the zoo and he would be alone. He would have to see his mother even at the risk of getting her disease. He was older and had grown a bit. He might be able to walk the thirty miles to the workhouse.

Remembering his mother set him thinking about stories they had read together of sailing ships and travels over the sea. He recalled a

favourite tale of a boy who was a stowaway. A
stowaway! Tod's mind began to spin. Why
couldn't he be a stowaway on Jumbo's ship? The
thought sent tingles through his body and a
giddy happiness into his heart. Thoughts led to
more thoughts, like an acrobat jumping from
loop to loop. He was small for his age and he
had slept for months in a sliver of a room in
Aunt Stubbs's attic. He could easily hide.

Tod's mind leapt with ideas. Mr Bartlett was
looking after his mother. He talked of moving
her to a hospital in London. Tod thought he
would write a letter to her telling her everything
and mail it on the day he sailed from England.
He could keep on writing to her from America.
He could save money for a visit if he got a job in
the Barnum circus.

That night, in the quiet secret of his attic,
Tod carefully unfolded paper, pen, envelope
and a stamp that he had bought in a nearby
shop. Spreading them over the floor beside his
mattress, he began to write the letter to his
mother.

Dear Mum,

Tomorrow I am going to stow away
on the ship that is taking Jumbo and
Scotty to America where they will work
for P.T. Barnum. I think I can get a job
with "The Greatest Show on Earth."

Maybe I can be a clown like Father. I
will save money and come home to visit
you.

Write to me at once at the Barnum
Circus, Madison Square Garden, New
York City.

I love you,

Tod

Tod put the letter carefully inside his school-
book. It would be ready for posting whenever
Jumbo sailed.

At the zoo Jumbo's crate was again rolled into
position outside the Elephant House. No one
was surprised that Jumbo had become more co-
operative and gentle since the announcement
of Scotty's new job, and on a pleasant day in
early March, Scotty led Jumbo with no tremors
and no objections through his crate, which was
open at both ends. He was led through the
crate again and again. Even Alice had her turn
tramping into the box.

The swelling number of visitors eyed the crate
with interest and worry. They began covering it
with names and messages. "Jumbo, don't go.
Jumbo, please stay." appeared in large scrawling
letters over the sides.

Tod watched every manoeuvre with sharp
eyes. He measured the crate. He could never
hide inside it. Jumbo's box was too small for two
passengers. Then he heard that a supply cart

filled with brushes and brooms and special equipment would follow Jumbo. He went to look at it carefully and decided that it would be his hiding place. He would crawl under the equipment. He would find a keeper's outfit and a large hat that Scotty had never seen before, and when he wiggled out of the supply crate and into the hull of the great ship no one would know him. According to stories he had read, even if he was caught on the ship, no one could send him back to England from the middle of the ocean.

Finally Tod settled on a plan, and during his noon visit with Jumbo he told the elephant every detail. He would leave the letter to his mother with Aunt Stubbs to be posted on the day he left. He hadn't been sure that she could read until one day he left one of his precious school-books on the table near his bowl of porridge. When he returned that evening he found the wizened old woman crouched over her chair with her face buried in the book as she slowly turned the pages. She hardly looked up when he ate his porridge and climbed to his attic room.

That night he printed a note in large letters on a piece of cardboard. It read:

I am leaving. Thank you for the room and the porridge. My mother is very

sick in the workhouse. Please post this
letter to her. You can keep my school-
book. I am sending my friend Colin to
live in your attic and help with your
chores.

Tod

It had occurred to Tod that his friend Colin
would be overjoyed with a warm room and regular food. He would write to him too just before
leaving.

11

It was a tug-of-war at the Zoological Gardens! On one side were eighteen thousand visitors who arrived at the zoo the day before Jumbo was now scheduled to depart.

They were a surging chorus pleading for their "beloved Jumbo's" right to remain on English soil.

"Three cheers for Jumbo!" the crowd shouted in a crescendo, and then pelted the elephant with peanuts and buns.

The thousands of visitors filled the Gardens, covering paths, flower beds and the cages of all the smaller animals. They swept through the zoo like a gale, blowing men, women and children towards the Elephant House and Jumbo.

On the other side of this tug-of-war were the astonished Fellows of the Zoological Gardens. They knew there was no stopping the approaching departure of the giant Jumbo. He had to go. Even Scotty agreed, now that he was leaving.

Tod remained silent. No one but Jumbo must know that he planned to leave too.

It was hard for Tod to hide his growing excitement about being a stowaway. He pretended sadness when the other sweepers and cleaners pleaded for Jumbo to stay. One evening he wrote a note on a scrap of paper for Aunt Stubbs to read. He wanted to share the crisis at the zoo with someone. The note said:

My friend Jumbo is leaving the zoo.

The old woman shook her head and wiped her eyes and gave Tod an extra bowl of stew. She, too, had read the daily papers.

The gale of visitors disrupted schedules. Food was delivered late. Lions roared impatiently. Bears growled with hunger. Monkeys chattered with disapproval and all the parrots screeched. In the noisy confusion, the Arab keeper of the hippopotamus, Obaysch, shook his fist at the disorder and cried that he was glad Mr Scott and Jumbo were leaving. Even Mr Bartlett cut off his visits to the Elephant House. He feared for his safety in all the turmoil.

At the Elephant House, Tod tried to remain calm. Scotty gave him detailed instructions for the departure day. He would follow Jumbo in his crate along the road from the Gardens to St Katharine's Docks. Then he would be on hand for the loading of Jumbo's box onto a barge that would float down the Thames River to Millwall Dock where Jumbo would be lifted by a crane onto the great steamer, the *Assyrian Monarch.*

"This part of the trip might take a long time," Scotty predicted. "At all times, Tod, see that Jumbo is fed and watered." Then he looked at Tod with genuine sadness.

"It's too bad you can't come on board ship," he said. "Jumbo and I will miss you, lad."

Tod was surprised and pleased by Scotty's guarded words of affection. They were like tears and hugs from anyone else.

Only Jumbo was at peace on the day before leaving. He ambled with swinging steps back and forth behind his iron fence. There was happiness in his small laughing eyes as he watched the friendly people press forward to touch his trunk and hand him the best treats he had ever eaten. Now that he was well again, the Elephant House in the Zoological Gardens was a small but splendid home for Jumbo, filled with food and care and love.

Dusk came early on Jumbo's last day at the zoo and Tod left quickly for Aunt Stubbs's cottage. She was asleep in her chair when he came in so he climbed quickly up the stairs to his tiny "dry space." He tucked the picture of his mother and father and himself inside his favourite school-book. Then he tightly folded one shirt and one pair of trousers and tied them, along with the book, into a small knot inside his mother's shawl. He planned to slip away in the middle of the night because Aunt Stubbs would stop him in the morning to do his chores. The note would tell her why he was leaving. Her deafness was a blessing. Even if he tripped going down the stairs, she wouldn't hear him.

Tod tried to sleep, but he bounced about on the mattress like a jumping frog. It was no use staying longer. He finally crawled down the stairs with his bundle. He could hear Aunt Stubbs snoring in her bed near the kitchen. He propped the cardboard note, his other school-book and the letter to his mother against the porridge bowl on the table and crept out the door.

He felt a twinge of regret leaving the little house. It had been a safe shelter, and just the presence of Aunt Stubbs had been a comfort, even though she wasn't what he would call a true friend. He thought of her as a cautious friend who didn't know how to show affection. He wondered if the reason might be that her deafness had blocked out all loving sounds. He knew, though, that he could trust her to send the letter to his mother.

Tod was relieved to find the street empty of people and all the lanterns dimmed. Even the zoo was deserted and silent when he finally squeezed through the locked main gate. At the Elephant House there was also silence. Not wanting to disturb anyone, Tod crawled into Jumbo's empty crate and promptly fell asleep.

Tod was wakened before daylight by a rattling cab that jolted to a stop on the road nearby. An elderly lady, wearing a wide-brimmed hat that was looped about with feathers and ribbons, stepped from its door. She had evidently talked someone into opening the gate to let her in. She carried an overflowing basket of oranges, apples, bunches of grapes and tiny cakes. The weight of it had her puffing, for she was plump and wore a tightly laced bodice.

Scotty was also wakened by the noise and stumbled out of doors.

"I've brought our dear Jumbo a parting gift," the lady cried out in a high, lilting voice. "I travelled most of the night to get here before he is taken away." She wiped tears from her eyes.

Jumbo began banging against his door.

"I'll let Jumbo into his outdoor enclosure," Scotty grumbled. "You can 'and the basket to 'im through the fence."

The woman was delighted. She walked to the fence and held out the treats to Jumbo's waving trunk. He instantly grabbed the basket and began tossing the apples and oranges into his mouth as though he were starving. But he didn't like the grapes and threw them on the ground. Then he seized the basket, crushed it with his trunk and ate all of it, including the wooden handle and the streams of ribbons.

"What an ungrateful creature!" exclaimed the woman. But she quickly repented her harsh words when she looked at Jumbo's obviously pleased expression. "Perhaps he would like a leg of lamb better."

"Elephants don't eat meat," Tod managed to answer, although he was still half asleep.

"What can I bring him?" the woman began to sob.

"Some old birch brooms," Scotty growled, and led Jumbo back into the Elephant House.

The woman got into her cab and rode away sadly.

Even though she had silly ideas about elephants, Tod knew how she felt. He had seen her many times outside the iron fence, feeding Jumbo. She loved the big elephant just as he did.

As she drove away, Mr Newman arrived to help Scotty harness Jumbo. They saw Tod and asked him to carry in the chains from the supply room. Jumbo spread both ears into protesting fans when he heard the clanking, and he became alarmed when both Scotty and Mr Newman began wrapping the chains around his legs. Why was he being shackled again after so many days of freedom and attention? Jumbo balked. He jerked and twisted his body in protest. But this time Scotty calmed him and led him easily out of the Elephant House and into his crate. Jumbo didn't know that this was the last time he would walk from his beloved home in the Zoological Gardens.

Jumbo started striding through his box as he had been doing for many days and was startled when Scotty and Mr Newman stopped him midway. They quickly secured the chains to hooks on the sides of the walls and closed both doors. A three-foot gap at the top in the front was the only opening left for the elephant to see through and extend his trunk.

Jumbo trumpeted furiously and began rocking the crate until Tod, who was watching nearby, wondered if he might smash it into splinters. Blacksmiths and carpenters were called to add more iron bars and thicker wooden planks and to test the sturdy wheels beneath the crate. They were heckled by early-arriving visitors who still hoped that Jumbo would refuse to leave his home.

There was pounding and hammering, sweeping and cleaning, packing and feeding throughout the day, and it wasn't until late that night that ten powerful horses, harnessed two abreast, began slowly pulling Jumbo's massive crate through the gates of the Zoological Gardens onto the road that led to the docks. Even at this late hour, there were still groups of people on the streets who were cheering Jumbo on his journey.

Scotty told Tod to ride on the small platform at the back of Jumbo's crate. The jogging of the wheels made him drowsy. He had been given a woollen blanket to protect him against the frosty night and the early spring snow flurries that blew into his face. He ducked his head into the blanket's soft folds and went to sleep.

12

Tod slept fitfully through the night, waking off and on to watch drowsy people come to their windows to catch a last glimpse of Jumbo. He was fully wakened in the early morning by a sudden jolt that sent him sprawling off the crate's back platform. He stood up quickly and looked about.

The crate was being surrounded by heavy ropes, and a huge crane above his head was preparing to lift the box off the ground and lower it onto a barge that was waiting in the river beside them.

Tod panicked. The supply box would be raised next and he had to hide in it at once. Everyone's attention was focused on Jumbo's waving trunk and the lifting crane. Tod could see Scotty standing on the crate's front platform.

He grabbed his bundle and crept slowly to the back of the supply crate, crawling over the side and ducking down under the bags of hay. He pulled loaves of bread and some bags of apples over his head and waited. It wasn't long until he felt the tug of ropes and a breath-taking swish into the air, followed by a slow descent into the barge beside Jumbo and Scotty.

The barge rocked gently as it floated down the Thames River towards the sea. Tod peeked through the slit between the boards of his crate and saw an amazing sight. Hundreds of rowboats drifted along the river near Jumbo's crate, and they were filled with cheering spectators. The British ensign flapped from a high pole on Jumbo's barge and nearby he caught sight of the stars and stripes of the American flag waving from the stern of a tug. A rowboat just beside him had "Jumbo" painted in large letters on its side.

It was noon when the barge stopped not far from a towering ship. Tod shivered with both fear and excitement. He had to get on board this ship and not be seen until it was far from England.

The barge edged close to the steamer. Tod's head bumped against a bag of apples as both crates were swiftly lifted from the barge into the air and then lowered into the deep hold of the great ship.

Scotty was already on board and Tod could hear him clearly as he asked Mr Newman, who was also there, "When did Tod leave us? I didn't get to say goodbye."

Tod hadn't realized that the two men would

be so near. He was terrified that he might be discovered.

It was dark and musty in the hold and impossible for Tod to see, but he could hear Jumbo rumbling softly and Scotty saying, "Quiet, Jumbo—Good Jumbo—We're on the ship that will take us across the ocean to 'The Greatest Show on Earth.'"

Tod wanted desperately to step outside and join his friends, but he couldn't make a sound or shift his cramped position. It seemed like an unbearable length of time until Scotty finally spoke again and announced to Jumbo that he was leaving "to get a bite to eat." He assured the elephant that he would return soon and that new sweepers and cleaners would arrive and give him food and water.

Tod's heart pounded. The food Scotty was talking about would be taken from the supply crate where he was hiding. He had to get out of it at once. Clutching his bundle and some bread and apples, he crawled over the bags of hay and jumped to the floor. A member of the crew appeared nearby with a bucket of water and a dirty bag of laundry. Tod could see him clearly. Jumbo stretched out his trunk toward the man in a friendly greeting. The sailor was taken by surprise and gave the trunk a hard smack with his bag.

Jumbo drew back. He wasn't used to this kind of treatment and he was offended. He watched the man slyly as he finished his laundry. Then he reached out quickly with his trunk, picked up the clean clothes and threw them on the dirty floor of his crate. He swished the laundry back and forth in the sodden hay and threw the now filthy clothes back into the man's face.

The sailor was enraged. "You mean, dumb beast!" he cried, and he got ready to toss the bucket of dirty water into Jumbo's face when another man appeared.

"Do you know you're attacking Jumbo, the most famous elephant in the world?" he exclaimed.

"Jumbo!" the sailor with the washing shouted. He picked up his bucket and the dripping clothes and the two men hurried from the room.

Jumbo now saw Tod through the hole in his crate and squealed with excitement. He banged his body against his box. He stretched out his trunk as far as it would go and stroked his young friend's face.

Tod leapt into a high cartwheel.

"It's a secret that I'm here, Jumbo," he whispered. "I'll be nearby and I'll see you whenever Scotty leaves. I'll have to share your apples and bread."

A rattling noise sent Tod scurrying into a dark corner. Somewhere in the hold, portholes were being opened to let in light and air. The motors of the great ship began to churn. The anchor was heaved aboard and a piercing whistle shattered the air. Tod jumped and Jumbo trumpeted. Scotty came running.

Tod couldn't let anyone catch him now. He was determined to stay on board the ship. He crept softly from the dark corner, holding his bundle against him, and kept to the shadows, feeling his way along the walls until he came to a door. It opened into a sailors' bunkroom. There was no one in it, but there were several ship uniforms hanging along the walls.

Tod grabbed one of them and put it on. It wasn't a perfect fit, but he could wear it and it was warmer than his ragged shirt and knickers. He threw his worn, patched clothes out the open porthole.

He would have to get as far as he could from Jumbo's quarters. He headed away from the hold and walked along dark corridors and empty passages until he found another hold to hide in. It wasn't until he heard one of the sailors call, "We're out to sea," that he finally realized the ship was moving. Then he relaxed.

When darkness came, Tod crawled up a dimly lit stairway to the top deck where he gulped in lungfuls of fresh sea air. It was bracing and delicious.

On the open deck, Tod found a different world than the quarters below where Jumbo stayed. A shower of stars hung above his head like a diamond canopy. Couples in elegant clothes strolled along the deck near the rails. Rich black waves lapped against the ship's sides, and in the distance, far off to the west, Tod imagined a world of circuses, clowns and elephants.

Late in the evening, food—fish, cheese, thin slices of bread, small cakes—appeared on a linen-covered table. Passengers strolled by it, nibbling at the food sparingly. When no one was watching Tod ran to the table and was filling his cap with food when a waiter came along the deck. After nearly being caught, Tod decided not to take any more chances. For the rest of the trip he ate from Jumbo's storage crate, going to it late at night when only Jumbo was awake.

Going back to the deserted hold below, Tod found a sheltered corner near some pipes where a pile of discarded blankets had been dumped and seemingly forgotten. He took off his ship uniform, folded it carefully and wrapped himself in one of the blankets. This was where he spent most of his days and slept at night on the long voyage.

It was a lonely time for Tod. His thoughts were often about his mother, and when he pictured her in his mind she was never ill in bed. She was laughing or prodding him with questions from the school-books. Surely she would get well in the new hospital where Mr Bartlett was sending her. One night he had a horrible dream that he was caught by the police when the ship docked in America and he was sent back to England without even telling Jumbo goodbye. On days when heavy seas tossed the ship back and forth like some giant rocking horse and Tod was too seasick to eat, he just sat curled up in the dark.

Then, in the early hours of dawn on Easter morning, 1882, the motors of the *Assyrian Monarch* became silent. The ship lay off shore in New York's North River. Everyone on board raced for a view of the famous city; there was a buzzing expectation. Tod left his hiding place and went up to the deck with the others to disembark. His brown tousled hair had grown longer in the last few weeks and he pulled it down over his eyes, hoping to avoid being recognized.

The sailors stood at attention. An announcement had just been made that the great showman, P.T. Barnum, was approaching the ship by tug. Tod forgot he was supposed to avoid drawing attention to himself and strained forward, pushing his hair back from his forehead and his eyes. Jumbo's crate was being lifted out of the hold so that his new owner could meet him.

"Mammoth, colossal Jumbo," as Mr Barnum was describing him in all the circus posters, had grown accustomed to ship life. He had made friends with the crew. Scotty and Elephant Bill Newman were his constant companions. But

Jumbo missed Tod and wondered why he no longer fed him or swept around him.

Now suddenly Jumbo was being lifted into the air again and he didn't like it. He banged to and fro until Scotty came to his side to quiet him.

The excitement of something grand and momentous spread like a sparking current up and down the ship as the seventy-year-old circus celebrity walked on board with sweeping steps. His white curly hair was lit by the afternoon sun and his piercing blue eyes, shielded by bushy white eyebrows, looked about quickly. They gave instant approval to his newest attraction for "The Greatest Show on Earth."

Barnum reached for Jumbo's trunk and in a booming voice proclaimed, "A circus must have clowns, peanuts and elephants. The greatest of these is elephants and Jumbo is the greatest elephant in the world!"

Everyone cheered and Jumbo bellowed.

Cheers erupted from the shore. Nearby tugs and other vessels blew their whistles. Jumbo trumpeted again and again.

As Jumbo turned his head to follow with his eyes a man carrying a tray of buns, he saw Tod in the crowd and recognized him at once. He began to wave his trunk in excited circles. Scotty also recognized Tod and looked completely shocked.

Tod walked slowly towards Mr Barnum and

Jumbo. He felt crushed and humiliated. He thought he had been so near to escaping to Barnum's circus. Now he would surely be returned to England and he might never see Jumbo again.

Scotty stepped forward and began to explain. "The boy is Tod Tolliver. He was the cleaner and sweeper for Jumbo at the Zoological Gardens in London. He must have slipped onto the ship and stowed away."

For a second, Mr Barnum turned his blue eyes on Tod and again they appeared to give instant approval.

"A circus can use a strong, healthy boy who is willing to work," he said quietly. He pushed the whole thing aside with a flourish of his hand, as if it had all been settled.

Tod bent down in his best circus bow before Mr Barnum and waved his cap across his chest.

PART III

13

The smile on Tod's thin face curved upward like a bright new moon. The giant of circuses—P.T. Barnum himself—had said that he could work in the circus!

Mr Barnum bowed to everyone on the deck and swept his tall silk hat in an arc across his chest. He prepared to go but turned back for a last look at Jumbo.

"Here stands one of the most powerful animals on the face of the earth and one of the most gentle," the showman mused. Then in a ringing voice he announced, "But P.T. Barnum will see that *he becomes the unrivalled giant in the World of Sawdust and Spangles!*" The renowned circus promoter smiled at everyone and left for the shore.

There was silence. No one was surprised by Mr Barnum's quick departure. It was known that he played almost no part in the daily preparations for the circus. It was his genius to find and advertise sensational exhibits.

Elephant Bill laughed and said to Scotty and Tod, "I hear that old Barnum has put an elephant to work ploughing a field on his farm in Connecticut. The keeper who leads him up and down is dressed in an oriental costume and Barnum makes certain that this spectacle takes place next to the railway track that runs straight to New York City."

"But why?" Scotty was puzzled. He knew nothing about this new world of make-believe, excitement and promotion.

Tod laughed. "I know why he's doing it. He's really promoting elephants, especially our Jumbo."

Scotty was still puzzled, but he turned to Tod, grabbed his hand and shook it with obvious pleasure. He was glad to see the boy, even though he said, "Being a stowaway is risky business, Tod. You shouldn't have done it."

Tod didn't agree, so he stared at the ground and gave no answer.

The attention of the circus staff now turned to the task of lifting, tugging, feeding, tending and cajoling Jumbo. Scotty and Mr Newman were in charge and Tod was put to work as Jumbo's first sweeper and cleaner.

When Scotty disappeared for a moment to chat with another circus trainer, Jumbo grabbed Tod's sailor hat and tossed it overboard. Tod howled and pretended he was going to somersault over the rail after it, but Jumbo swept him away from the rail with his trunk. Tod stroked the elephant's crinkled, leathery nose.

"Oh, Jumbo," Tod told his friend in high-pitched excitement. "You will love the circus. I've seen pictures of Madison Square Garden. The room is so big you'll have space to stretch and walk as fast as you like. The ceiling is almost as high as the sky. Acrobats will swing through the air on ropes up there. The bands will play and you'll march with the horses and the clowns and there will be lions and tigers in rolling cages." Tod's face was radiant.

He drew closer to Jumbo's crate and whispered. "Think of it. My father was a circus man. Now I will be a circus man too. I just wish that Mum could be here."

It was late afternoon when Jumbo reached the southern tip of Manhattan Island. A crowd of two thousand people was waiting to welcome the famous new immigrant to America. Jumbo's trunk waved through the side of his crate. He trumpeted now and then as if in answer to the whistles of the tugs and the cheers of the spectators. Tod stared at the buildings of New York with awe. He could hardly believe he was here.

The circus people thought they had prepared for moving big Jumbo through the city streets. But the huge weight of the elephant and his crate astonished them. Sixteen horses and scores of men were called into action to pull on a long rope attached to the crate. Two of

Barnum's circus elephants, Gipsy and Chief, were brought from Madison Square Garden to push with their heads against the back of Jumbo's crate.

Midnight struck as Jumbo was slowly pulled and pushed down Broadway in pouring rain. In the half-light of daybreak the team of workers at last came to a stop at the open doors of Madison Square Garden, the great indoor stadium which housed the Barnum and Bailey Circus. Scotty comforted Jumbo and directed the operations. Tod fed his friend with the freshest hay and juiciest apples.

When the door of the crate was finally pulled open and Jumbo took his first careful step onto American soil and into the circus building, Scotty whispered into his ear. Jumbo stretched and then knelt and fell on his side, rolling back and forth and waving his trunk happily into the air.

The circus folk who had gathered to greet Barnum's newest purchase understood. Jumbo was doing something denied him for many days on board the ship.

Trained circus people gathered around and surveyed Barnum's newest exhibit with astonishment.

"He's the tallest elephant I've ever seen!"

"He seems to be walking on stilts."

"He's intelligent looking."

"Don't rush him. Treat him gently," Scotty advised.

Jumbo at last rose to his feet and Tod watched his eager eyes survey the vast building with its endless track that circled the floor and the high ceiling that was like a miniature sky. He trumpeted loudly.

Tod smiled. "I think he's saying, 'At last I've found a building big enough for me.'"

Scotty led Jumbo slowly around the track and finally into a big room where he would have his own private quarters away from the herd of thirty performing elephants. There was a rail around it to restrain the public waiting to see him. His hind leg was fastened with a chain tethered to a sturdy wooden stake in the ground. The circus workers were friendly, and Jumbo moved forward towards them. The stake slipped from the ground as if it were a toothpick.

Blacksmiths were summoned. The fence was built higher. The stake was forged into an iron bar. Tod piled hay around Jumbo and handed him fresh buns for a welcoming treat. He turned a spirited cartwheel and was about to do another when he felt Scotty's hand on his shoulder.

Circus hands began to bustle with growing speed to finish their tasks. There was an excited tingle in the air and Tod could sense that it was time for the afternoon performance to begin. The blare of brass instruments and the rolling of drums were like flashes of lightning foretelling a momentous event. Above them rose the excited voices of the crowd coming in.

The people surged into the Menagerie where the animals were being exhibited before the show began. They wanted to see Jumbo. Barnum's ballyhoo, billboards and exaggerated speeches were paying off. The crowd wasn't disappointed. The giant Jumbo was the largest animal they had ever seen.

Jumbo was pleased to have crowds of people surrounding him again. It must have reminded him of his happy days in the Zoological Gardens. There were lots of peanuts, fruit and candies.

Mr Newman was pleased with Jumbo's friendliness and with Scotty's ability to prepare him with his secret cues for all these new experiences. He even complimented Tod for his expert sweeping and cleaning.

"Very soon," Mr Newman announced with a show of pride, "Jumbo will enter the circus proper. A regal robe is being designed for him to wear and you, Scott, will have a red coat with sparkling buttons and a velvet hat that rides high on your head."

He turned to Tod. "You will help get Jumbo ready for the great event. I hear you used to ride on Jumbo in London. We may decide later to have you ride on his back in the opening parade."

Tod skipped and hopped around the corridors of the Menagerie. He was cartwheeling down an empty hall when he heard a call. He walked to an open door and looked into "Clown Alley," the special dressing room for the clowns. A man with a painted sad face in baggy pants and floppy shoes was looking back at him.

"So, we have a new boy who perhaps needs to be in clown training," he said, circling his head up and down and then backwards and forwards. "Be here at six o'clock tomorrow morning and ask for Fosset. We'll see if you might qualify."

Tod couldn't believe what he had just heard. Was it possible that he might join a clown-training class in the mornings before his work with Jumbo began?

That night in the room where Tod would sleep with other circus workers, he sat on the side of his cot and wrote a letter to his mother. It went on for pages and pages. Writing it was like having her in the room with him and talking to her, and he didn't want that feeling to end.

14

Delicious smells of steaming coffee and frying bacon woke Tod before sunrise. He jumped from his cot and pulled on a green circus outfit that had been laid out for him. Others were heading for breakfast. Tod followed them and found a place on the bench of a long table. He filled his plate at once with hot pancakes, ham and eggs and several strips of bacon. The sights and sounds of the circus people around him took Tod's thoughts back to the small travelling show in England he had been part of with his mother and father. He almost expected to see them sitting across the table from him. He wished that they were really there.

"The circus is a family," his mother always said.

After eating, Tod decided to go straight to Clown Alley and talk with the sad-faced clown named Fosset. He bounded down a corridor and banged into Elephant Bill Newman, almost knocking him down.

"You're running in the wrong direction, Tod," the older man said. "The Menagerie is behind you."

Tod burst forth with a report of his encounter with Fosset and his hope of being accepted in the early-morning clown class.

"But I thought you were devoted to the elephant. I thought you wanted to spend all your time with him. You even stowed away on the *Monarch* just to be near him." Mr Newman was obviously puzzled.

"Jumbo is my best friend in the world," Tod said loyally. Then in quick detail he told Mr Newman of his father, the clown, and about his mother, the circus teacher.

"So that's the reason for all the somersaulting," Mr Newman smiled. "You come from a circus family."

"I'll talk with Fosset," he added, looking at the serious, thin-faced young Tod with new interest. "But we'll have to postpone your meeting with him for a week. Right now, Tod, we need you to help get Jumbo ready for the circus this afternoon."

"This afternoon!" Tod jumped into the air. He raced back to the Menagerie and found Scotty being fitted in his new circus outfit. He was holding a large mirror in front of his face and twisting his greased moustache into ringlets on either end. He seemed pleased with himself, but anxious about Jumbo. He was especially relieved to see Tod.

"As soon as they finish fixing this bloomin' outfit, we'll work on Jumbo," he said. "Feed him, Tod. Scatter fresh hay. Then it's hosin' and scrubbin' and cuttin' his toenails. We'll even take him once around the Hippodrome ring just for exercise."

"We'll polish him until he shines, Mr Scott," Tod stood up as proud and tall as his thin, wiry figure would allow.

Jumbo would lead the parade with Scotty beside him, and when they stepped into the arena they would be introduced by the ringmaster.

Scotty was breathless as he outlined these coming events. For a silent, retiring man of few words, the noisy razzmatazz of the circus preparations all around him was unsettling.

"When the parade ends," Scotty continued, "we'll walk to one side of the middle ring and watch the whole show. I want you there, Tod, to help us."

Tod felt proud. Scotty had never asked him for this kind of help before. Then he remembered once when he had first started working at the London Zoo Scotty had mocked his spins and cartwheels and his talk of the circus. It must be hard for Scotty, he thought, who had been the best elephant trainer in the Gardens to live in a place that he didn't understand.

The busy morning ended abruptly with the beating of drums and the trumpet calls to attention. Noisy crowds surged into the Menagerie to see the "Great Jumbo."

Jumbo perked up his fan-like ears. There were even more people, peanuts and candy than the day before. But Jumbo was not only interested in food, he poked out his long trunk over the fence just for the loving caresses of the children.

The trumpeting grew louder and the drum beats more urgent.

Elephant Bill Newman took charge.

"Line up the elephants in a trunk-to-tail formation with Jumbo in the lead," he shouted.

Thirty swaying, lumbering elephants in single file each grabbed the tail of the elephant in front with his trunk. Tod knew that this formation would keep the animals in line and their trunks out of mischief.

Earlier Mr Newman had told Scotty that there would be no rider or howdah on Jumbo's back for this first performance, and no elephant would grab his tail.

It had also been announced by Barnum, and the words passed along to every member of the circus staff: "Jumbo is the patriarch of the elephant herd. He will walk alone like a giant. He will not do tricks because he is interesting just the way he is. Nor will he do any haulage work, because he was never trained for this. Jumbo is the greatest star in the circus!"

Spirited music blared from the full brass

band. A red satin robe covered with shimmering silver sequins was thrown over Jumbo's back. Scotty, in his bright new uniform, stood proudly by his side. Tod was whisked off quickly by a circus hand to a seat in front of the centre ring in the Hippodrome where Jumbo and Scotty would eventually stand.

A whistle blew. A hush fell over the crowd as the ringmaster cried out through his silver horn. He stood majestically on a raised platform in the centre of the arena.

"Laaadeeezzz and gentlemen, boys and girls, the Barnum and Bailey Circus—The Greatest Show on Earth—is about to begin!"

Tod filled his lungs with the circus smells of freshly sprinkled sawdust, tanbark, taffy, popcorn and parched "goobers"—roasted peanuts.

Another whistle blew, followed by a deafening roll of drums.

"Laaadeeezzz and gentlemen, boys and girls," the ringmaster shouted again, "here he is! The animal you have been waiting to see, the mightiest animal in all the world, JUMBO!"

The sequin-robed Jumbo entered the ring to the rolling of the drums and the shouting of the crowd of people who had risen to their feet.

At Scotty's command, Jumbo lifted his trunk and let out a full-throated trumpet. The crowd cheered again and again.

The resounding full brass band began to play "The Entry of the Gladiators." Jumbo's slow, graceful, swinging steps kept perfect time to the music as he began his first appearance in the circus.

"Jumbo is a giant just like Mr Barnum said," Tod told himself as he rose to his feet with wide-eyed wonder.

The long row of thirty smaller elephants followed their patriarch's rhythmic steps, and at the end of the line, straining to reach the tail of the elephant in front of him, was a midget elephant called Tom Thumb. His small pudgy body brought peals of laughter from the children.

The music played on as rolling gilded cages filled with growling tigers and roaring lions passed by. Behind them rode sparkly-costumed women riding bareback on white horses. Tumbling white-faced clowns with painted mouths and eyes and baggy clothes came next, falling over one another and into the aisles. Some were on high stilts.

The parade ended just as the three rings began to fill with performers. In the first ring, wild animals were released from their cages. A whip cracked but never touched them. A wire cage was thrown up around the snarling creatures to protect the audience, but the trainer stood alone, bare to the waist with his muscles flexing as he faced the animals with only a whip.

In another ring, spine-chilling music began as tight-rope walkers balanced high in the air, riding bicycles and carrying passengers on their shoulders as they crossed the wire. Without warning, Mademoiselle Zazel was shot out of a cannon and caught by a man hanging from a swinging trapeze.

Tod grew dizzy trying to watch everything.

The centre ring with the elephant act, however, grabbed all of Jumbo's attention. It began with the "Leaps," a performance of teamwork between elephants and acrobats. Runners leaped over a line of elephants from a running board, turning somersaults before landing. Some elephants rolled balls. A small group danced in a circle to fast music and several sat on stools with their front legs held out like arms.

Jumbo trumpeted again and again as he watched them. But it was the last act that involved his attention totally. He didn't move and his eyes sparkled when Tom Thumb, the midget elephant, walked into the ring on his hind legs with his trainer. The tiny elephant picked up a bell with his trunk and rang for a waiter, who was a white-faced, smiling, rollicking clown. He carried a tray with food, two glasses and a bottle of coloured water. Tom Thumb seized the bottle in his trunk and drank it.

The waiter went away to get another bottle and the performance was repeated several times, until finally Tom Thumb rose from the table, ate everything on it including the paper plates, and, holding his stomach, staggered out of the ring. The audience laughed hilariously.

Jumbo was transfixed. As the act ended and the audience began leaving the arena, Jumbo pulled and tugged at Scotty and insisted on following the midget elephant. When they met, Jumbo lowered his head almost to the ground to look into the eyes of his new-found friend. Their admiration for each other was instant and they refused to be separated.

Mr Newman and Scotty talked about it. Why not let them live side by side? They could welcome visitors together in one enclosure in the Menagerie. It would be a great attraction.

"And from now on Tom Thumb will follow Jumbo in the opening parade," said Mr Newman.

Tod was fascinated by this new friendship, but he was even more fascinated by the white-faced clown who was the waiter in the act. Someday he would like to be a clown working with an elephant in Barnum's great circus.

15

Tod was jubilant. After only a few weeks in the circus he was going to clown school every morning. Fosset, a stern taskmaster but the best clown teacher in the circus, had arranged it. Tod could imagine his own father dancing in loops and twirls if he were alive and could be with him now. He vowed that he would try to be the best student in the class and he began to dream that someday soon he would have his own clown trunk, his own make-up kit and his own act in the circus performance.

Like everyone else in the circus, Tod would have other things to do. In the afternoon, he would tend Jumbo and stand beside him during the afternoon performance. He was also going to attend the circus school for two hours in the morning after clown practice.

"Our young folks must have book learning added to sawdust learning," Fosset declared. The tall, severe man never seemed to rest. He

and his wife were the parents of three performing children. They, too, had grown up as circus
children. Their youngest son, Jip, about Tod's
size and age, was a juggler. When Tod met him
he was balancing a hoop on his head and juggling three balls in his hands.

"Jip will teach you juggling," his father said.
He caught one of the balls and showed Jip how
to toss it higher.

A slightly older sister, Jenny, danced ballet.
She spun and twirled on her toes with the light-
ness of an airborne fairy. Her straight black hair
knotted tightly at the back of her head and her
dark sparkling eyes gave her a dramatic, flashing beauty, Tod thought.

"You must meet Momma," Jip said with pride
when he paused from his juggling. "She's the
greatest performer of us all. She swings on her
trapeze high above the centre ring and then
hangs by her teeth and whirls."

Tod was impressed, but not as impressed as
he was when he met Arto, the oldest son, who
was dressed in the costume of a white-faced
clown. Tod recognized him at once. He was the
clown in the act with Tom Thumb, whom Tod
had been watching for weeks.

Tod could see that Fosset was proud of his
performing children.

"I've trained them since birth to be great stars
in the circus," he said, pulling at his small,
pointed beard. Tod thought he noted a steely

sound in Fosset's voice. It made him wonder if Fosset might make it difficult for anyone to compete with his own children.

Elephant Bill Newman found it hard to convince Scotty that Tod should have clown training. It was difficult for Scotty to unbend and admit that he was beginning to enjoy the fun and excitement of the circus. He had to concede, however, that Jumbo was happy.

Tod tried to explain to him. "The clowns make people laugh after all those dangerous acts on the trapeze, Mr Scott."

Scotty wasn't convinced.

"Fosset calls the clowns the ambassadors of goodwill," Tod looked straight at Scotty. "He says people have to have jokes just to be able to live in this world."

Scotty was beginning to listen.

"And Mr Barnum says," Tod continued, looking slyly at his boss, "that elephants and clowns are the pegs on which a circus hangs."

"Well, I agree with him as far as elephants are concerned," Scotty answered. This time he laughed. "I guess bein' born into a circus family makes you different from me."

Tod did begin to feel that he was once again a member of a family—the circus family. Jip became his friend as well as his teacher, and they often ate their meals together.

But the excitement of his clowning lessons did not lessen Tod's eagerness to care for and talk with Jumbo. He shared all his new experiences and all his worries, as he always had, with his best friend in the world.

As Tod and Jumbo stood side by side each afternoon in front of the centre ring with Scotty, after Jumbo's spectacular parade around the Hippodrome track, Tod watched only the clowns. He learned by heart each gesture Arto made in his act with Tom Thumb. Tod thought how he might improve the act, how he might paint a funnier face on himself and make the children laugh until they rolled off their seats.

Jumbo looked only at the elephant acts. He saved all his trumpeting and squealing for Tom Thumb.

At the end of each busy day, Tod lay on his cot and wrote down all his experiences in long letters to his mother. He mailed them regularly, but she still wasn't well enough to answer them.

Preparations and talk buzzed among the circus folk about leaving to "go on the road." The season was ending at Madison Square Garden and the entire circus would soon be packed into long trains and travel to cities and small towns in the eastern United States and Canada. There would be two performances each day under the largest tent in the world—"The Big Top." If a letter from his mother didn't come soon, Tod wondered how it would ever catch up with him. He raced daily to the post box hoping to find it there.

Tod and his friend Jip found a large map of North America and drew "X" marks over every town and city where they would stop. Talk of crossing the border and performing in Canada created special excitement, for many people had never been there.

Even Scotty became excited.

"Can you believe it?" he said one day as he and Tod were brushing Jumbo's back, "The circus train has a hundred carriages and freight cars that are made up into four separate trains!"

Tod laughed, "I heard a clown say that Mr Barnum is warning the public that they should come to see Jumbo now before he grows too big for the railway tunnels."

It was Jip who told Tod about the car that the Pennsylvania Railroad Company had made especially for Jumbo to travel in.

"It will be called 'Jumbo's Palace Car'!" Jip jumped about with excitement as he threw three hoops into the air. "It's being painted crimson and gold. . . . It'll have huge double doors in the middle so that Jumbo can step in and out. . . . It'll hold water and food and loads of clean straw. . . ." Jip, out of breath, dropped one of his hoops.

Another young clown finished the description. "And Mr Scott will have his bunk near the front of the car so Jumbo can even reach him with his trunk."

"I wonder where I'll travel?" Tod asked a little wistfully, wanting to be both with the clowns and with Jumbo.

"Father wants you to be with the clowns," Jip answered. "We practise our acts, sometimes, even when the train is rolling."

As the day for leaving Madison Square Garden approached, Tod was both worried and excited. No letter had come from his mother. But he was excited because Mr Newman had announced that Tod would ride in the howdah on Jumbo's back in all the small-town circus parades. "The animals and performers will march down Main Street just before the afternoon performances," Elephant Bill said.

"Riding in the parades," Tod told Jumbo later, "will be the next best thing to acting in a real live performance under the Big Top."

Lately, as Tod practised clowning until his back ached, he began to realize that he was behind in his training compared to most of the other young boys. He wanted desperately to take part in the daily shows, but there were so many others who had practised longer. Tod remembered all the clowning he had done in front of Jumbo at the Zoological Gardens, but there had never been anyone to teach him there.

In the final days at Madison Square Garden Jumbo had become so tame and gentle that rumours began to spread that he might take children for rides on his back again as he had done for so many years in the London Zoo.

Tod was pleased. He talked about the old days with Scotty.

"Remember, Mr Scott, the first time I rode on Jumbo's back and you led us around by Mum's refreshment stand?"

Suddenly, with the mention of his mother's name, Tod's happiness left him.

"And how is she?" Scotty asked.

"I haven't had a letter for a long time," was the only answer Tod could give.

"Then we must write to Mr Bartlett and get a report." Scotty seemed concerned.

At last there was only one day left until the great Barnum and Bailey Circus would leave New York City and roll by train through the countryside.

Tod raced to clean Jumbo's enclosure as well as Tom Thumb's on the last afternoon at Madison Square Garden. He fed both elephants and laughed as they bumped and tugged playfully with one another. Their friendship was the talk of the circus. Jolly little Tom Thumb only measured as high as Jumbo's knee.

Tod hurried to the post box, hoping to have his mother's letter before leaving. There was a letter and it had his name on it. But it wasn't from his mother. It was from Mr Bartlett. Tod tore it open. The letter read:

Dear Tod:

Your mother is now in a good hospital with better care, but she is very ill. At the moment she is not well enough to write. She will, no doubt, write as soon as she is better.

I send my regards to you and Mr Scott.

A.D. Bartlett

16

Tod kept Mr Bartlett's letter in his pocket, but it felt like a very heavy weight. How could he jump and whirl in the air with all the excitement going on around him when he carried such a burden?

Tod went with Jip to see Jumbo's Palace Car and thought it as grand as the palace of a real king or queen. He was happy to discover that he was going to bunk each night with Jip in the clown coach of the circus train. Many of his cherished dreams seemed to be coming true. But he wanted to share them with his mother. He and she had dreamed them together.

Tod had a strange, disconnected feeling. He was seeing colour, wonder and magic, but his heart was heavy with sadness. He took the letter to Jumbo during Scotty's lunch time and held it in front of the elephant's small eyes.

"Mum is very ill," he told his friend. "She's too ill to even write me a letter."

"Oh, Jumbo," Tod burst into tears. "She could die from the sickness. I haven't seen her for such a long time."

Jumbo stroked Tod's face with his trunk.

Tod wandered through Clown Alley where the clowns were carefully packing their trunks. He knew from the old days with his father how special these trunks were. They held make-up and costumes. They could be turned into make-up stands or even dining tables in one second. And it was a sacred rule among clowns that none of them could act or dress or use make-up the same way as another clown. They had to be original.

As Tod strolled along he noticed a middle-aged clown with greying hair and a face as gloomy as a storm cloud. He sat with his head buried in his hands. Tall Mr Fosset hovered beside him, patting the older man's shoulder. Tod saw Arto nearby and stopped to ask the reason for the man's unhappiness.

"His wife was buried this afternoon," Arto answered softly. "She fell from a trapeze last week and broke her neck."

"How can he go on the trip tomorrow?" Tod worried.

"It isn't easy," Arto replied as he kept on packing. His dark eyes were sober. "All of us in the circus learn that pains, troubles and heartaches must be put aside for the show, especially when we enter the ring. All that matters is the act and doing our best. Think of the thousands who'd be disappointed if we didn't. The show must go on, Tod. The show must go on."

The words stuck in Tod's mind as he hurried to his cot and packed his own small bag. Thoughts twisted about inside his head when he tried to sleep. He couldn't believe that his mother might die. He had to keep on believing that he would see her again.

The eerie whistle of a train—the circus train—called through the darkness. It beckoned to distant places and new adventures. Tod knew he was going to follow it, and with this assurance he fell asleep.

Early morning came like a whirlwind, with packing and moving and shouting and the roars and screams of the wild animals. Tod found himself humming an old tune that he had heard his father sing on the days of setting up and breaking down their small English circus. "Fast-paced—No waits—No breaks—Fast-paced."

There was no confusion among the performers, other workers and animals as they boarded the long winding trains of one hundred cars. Coaches, stock cars for the animals and double flat cars that carried the circus wagons were all in readiness. A stocky man, the principal organizer, barked orders in the manner of a general in an army.

Jumbo led the elephants in trunk-to-tail formation until he came to the glittering Palace

Car where he would live. Here he would eat and sleep in spacious comfort. Scotty would be in his own compartment at the front of it, and Tom Thumb would be nearby. The other elephants were housed in less elaborate quarters.

It was now agreed by all the animal trainers that when Jumbo was with Scotty he was obedient and good-humoured. He saved his playful pranks and hat-grabbing tricks for Tod.

The shrill train whistle silenced everyone. "All aboard," a conductor called. Steam hissed from the engines and Tod and Jip grabbed the armrests of their coach seats to prepare for the sudden jerk of starting.

The train chugged slowly, then gathered speed and was soon in the country. The two boys pressed their faces against the window to watch the endless fields stretch like great green and brown carpets across the land. They counted white horses and spot-faced cows and waved to farm children gathered along the railway tracks. Night came and their seats were turned into beds. They slept soundly, their bodies bumping back and forth as the long speeding train turned and twisted on its way to the town that would be its first stop.

"Time to get up," Fosset's voice rang through the clowns' coach before dawn.

"You, Tod, will join Jumbo and Mr Scott to prepare for the parade," he called out. No one disobeyed Fosset.

Fast-paced—No breaks— Tod thought sleepily and then jumped from his bed. Some of the elephants were already lumbering past his train window. They would all walk the two miles to a weed-covered lot that was at this moment being transformed into a city of tents.

Tod joined Jumbo and Scotty as they stepped down a wooden ramp from the Palace Car. Tom Thumb trotted instantly to Jumbo's side. Jumbo nudged Tod playfully with his trunk and then trumpeted with happiness to be in the free, open country. Other wild animals added their cries as their box car doors opened.

An eager group of local boys gathered along the tracks. One of them screamed "Jumbo," and in a single unit the others clamoured towards the elephants. Scotty held them back with a bull-hook, and warned them there might be stampedes or tramplings if they didn't keep their distance.

Jumbo swung his trunk freely in the fragrant air and pounded his feet on the soft earth. As they drew near the circus lot, Tod was amazed. The cookhouse tent was already set up and the cooks were serving breakfast. Nearby in a narrow canvas lean-to was Clown Alley. Someday that's where I will go, Tod thought wistfully to himself as he looked down the row of trunks and costumes and painted faces.

Busy men and working elephants swarmed over the folds of canvas—the making of the Big

Top. Heavy stakes were hammered into the ground to support guy ropes. Great poles were erected. Within minutes, it seemed, the big tent billowed out in all directions.

"Heave it, weave it, shake it, move along there," the workers chanted.

Tod gasped as he looked inside. The huge space of Madison Square Garden had been transported to the farm lands. Ropes and wires for the trapeze and high-wire performances criss-crossed in webs and patterns from the top of the tent. The three rings of "The Greatest Show on Earth" appeared with freshly sprinkled sawdust to form a fragrant, earthy carpet. Next came the Hippodrome track where Jumbo would march at the head of the parade when the ringmaster announced, "The show is about to begin!" Hundreds of people would sit in the tiered seats being set up around the edges.

Tod marched with Jumbo and Scotty into a tent that was lower than the Big Top and long like a passageway. It was a stable, with stalls divided by wooden partitions and filled with clean, fresh straw.

Tod grabbed buckets of fresh water to scrub and water both Jumbo and Tom Thumb. Within minutes the red sequined robe was thrown over Jumbo and a gold-trimmed howdah was fastened to his back. Jumbo's small eye sparkled with pleasure.

"He's a true performer," a lion tamer exclaimed. "He belongs in the circus."

In another minute, Tod found himself transformed from a sweeper and cleaner into an oriental prince dressed in a glittering coat and a make-shift crown.

All the animals and performers that would make up the parade quickly formed into a long single line and started their march. The magnificent parade began to move slowly through the town. Jumbo, with Tod on his back, swung his enormous legs in perfect rhythm to the familiar marching music of the circus band. Little Tom Thumb obediently hung onto Jumbo's tail with his trunk.

The parade turned a corner and Tod could see the clowns behind him falling in and out of small wagons pulled by trained dogs. After them came the brightly costumed ladies standing on bareback horses with red plumes on their heads. Wild animals paced back and forth in their wheeled cages. A giraffe towered above the street-lamps of the town. And, at the end of the line, rode the calliope and its player, the massive strong man of the circus, Professor Burzardo. Tod liked the calliope best of all.

Two wagons were needed to carry the great steam-engine music machine with its series of whistles. It took all the strength of the heavy-set professor to force 120 pounds of steam pressure to start the music that could be heard as far away as ten miles. His strong fingers pressed over the keyboard as if he were merely playing the keys of a piano. The circus band became silent as the calliope ended the parade with one of Tod's favourite songs, "Wait Till the Clouds Roll By."

The parade turned to go back to Tent City and veered off Main Street onto a shady lane with rows of ancient elm trees. Tod found himself envying the stately houses with old people rocking and fanning themselves on wide-pillared front porches; and parents and children racing over green lawns in happy games and play. A young girl in a white linen dress rushed from her porch and threw Tod a bag of candy.

Shouts of "Jumbo, Jumbo" came from everywhere. Jumbo was the star attraction and he liked it.

Crowds of people followed the parade towards the Big Top for the afternoon performance. It was as though they had been sucked in by a huge vacuum machine and then blown into the three-ring arena.

A new sign greeted Jumbo and Tod as they entered the circus grounds:

BOYS AND GIRLS
—AFTER THE PERFORMANCE—
LINE UP FOR A RIDE
ON THE GREAT JUMBO'S BACK!

Tod was thrilled until he remembered again the London Zoo and his mother and his first ride on Jumbo's back. He had been so busy and excited that he had forgotten the letter.

A chill crept up Tod's spine. He had to admit that his mother might die in the hospital. But there was also a chance she could recover slowly. He could send his letters now to the new hospital address. He would also send his mother the address of the winter headquarters for Barnum's circus in Bridgeport, Connecticut. She would have the whole summer to answer him. But he would like to do something more for her than writing letters.

A new idea came to him. He was earning a small salary and he didn't have to spend it on a room or on food. He lived and ate in the circus. Why couldn't he begin to save most of his money and buy a steamship ticket for his mother to sail to New York City? The thought of this might help her get well. He would talk with Scotty about where to safely put the money.

The long circus train criss-crossed the eastern United States and crossed the border into Canada, giving hundreds of performances. Jumbo, the featured attraction, loved the children, the rides, the parades and the shouts of "Jumbo." He could have continued for a hundred more shows. But the performers and the staff were getting tired—even Tod was tired.

They were ready to head for their winter quarters and have a rest.

There was an icy chill in the wind that swirled about the circus train when it pulled into winter headquarters in Bridgeport. Some of the animals shivered as they walked the long distance from the train station to the large heated buildings which housed everyone at Barnum's enormous permanent winter site. Tod couldn't believe he was going to live for several months in this spacious comfort.

At first Jumbo was confused by the lack of crowds and treats, the spirited band music and the marching parades. But he began to enjoy the attention Scotty gave him "to bring my elephant back into first-rate condition." There were thorough scrubbings and brushings to make his hide shine. He had more food and could eat it at leisure. Scotty measured Jumbo and announced that he was still growing. Even his tusks were longer.

For Tod there was little rest. He was excited when he was assigned to live with the clowns. There were daily rehearsals of juggling, fencing, acrobatics, make-up and even dancing lessons from Jenny Fosset. He looked forward to these sessions. Jenny was strict and precise like her father. But unlike her father she was friendly and when the lesson was over she laughed and joked with Tod. He was beginning to think her smile was the most beautiful one in the circus.

Tod was determined to do his best in the clown classes. He desperately wanted to be chosen for an act in the coming season at Madison Square Garden.

During a difficult clown class, Tod found himself alone with Fosset while he waited for his turn to somersault.

"What will I do when we go back to Madison Square Garden, Mr Fosset?" Tod asked in an unsteady voice. "I want to be a clown in the rings."

"You will keep on riding on Jumbo's back in the opening parade around the Hippodrome," Fosset spoke hastily. "Keep working and practising on your clowning. Someday you will probably have your own trunk and your own clown face."

Tod's disappointment was deep, but he tried not to show it.

There was also book-learning school each afternoon for the circus boys and girls in a special room with desks, books and a blackboard. Tod was seated with the oldest students now. The first day, when he looked up and saw a small, pale man as his teacher, he thought at once of another teacher—his mother.

But Tod's thoughts about his mother were no longer filled with despair. They were edged with excitement. He had started to save money for her steamship ticket and Scotty had gone with him to open an account in a bank. He had written to his mother about this plan and she had answered. Her handwriting was still in weak, feathery strokes but this time the sentences were longer. She wrote:

> Dear Toddy:
>
> I am still very ill. But the news in your letters about your wonderful life in the circus with Jumbo keeps me alive from day to day. I look forward to the promise of a steamship ticket and a trip to Madison Square Garden, even if it takes a long, long time.
>
> I send my love,
> Mother

Tod took the letter immediately to Jumbo, whom he visited every day. Jumbo seemed to share the good news; he squealed and trumpeted.

More good news from England arrived when Scotty appeared with a letter from Aunt Stubbs. He spread the pages out on a table and gently rubbed his hand over them.

He smiled, "It says that the week after we pulled off shore on the *Assyrian Monarch* your young friend Colin came to live with her. She likes him and she helped him get a job at the zoo." He paused. "She's my only living relative."

Tod felt a rush of affection for the old woman who had given him shelter and food, and he was happy that Colin had found a home with her.

PART IV

17

Weeks slipped into months and then into more months until it became Jumbo's third year in the Barnum Circus. Tod was now fourteen. He was still small and thin but "as strong as steel," Fosset had to admit. Tod was eager and quick and a clown both in and out of his practice costume.

"Tod is a favourite in our circus," Elephant Bill Newman told Scotty one day. Scotty laughed. He still preferred the company of Jumbo over people.

As for Jumbo, he and Tom Thumb were inseparable. They often stood in their separate stalls with heads near each other and ears flapping as though they were having a long conversation.

With some quiet help from Scotty, the money in Tod's savings mounted until at last, there was enough for Molly's ticket. But she was still not well enough to travel. Only long days of rest could cure consumption. She wrote:

Send the fare, Toddy.
I will surprise you someday and sail!

    Your mother

Tod responded at once and mailed the fare.

The performances that season were proclaimed to be the largest and the best in
Madison Square Garden's history. Jumbo continued to be the star. Tod rode gallantly on
Jumbo's back in the opening parade wearing
a new sparkling robe. But he still wanted to
act with the clowns. Jip had been given a role
in the centre ring with his twirling hoops.
Jenny danced on the back of a galloping
white horse. Arto and Tom Thumb now had
two acts instead of one. Other clowns who
were Tod's age appeared in the rings. He continued his clown classes daily. But Fosset con-
centrated on the young beginners who were
children of the circus families. He had little
time for Tod.

Soon the Barnum and Bailey Circus was on
the road again with double their usual requests
for appearances. Jumbo drew larger and larger
crowds. His gentle personality and enormous
size captured the hearts and minds of thousands.

One evening late in the summer tour, the circus train pulled into the busy railroad town of
St Thomas, Ontario. Tod realized that he might
have lived near a town just like this one if his

mother's plan to send him to a farm in Canada had worked out. He shuddered at the thought of never being in the circus and losing all contact with Jumbo and Scotty.

The train screeched to a stop on a side line next to the main railroad track. Tod jumped from his coach into the railway yard. The circus manager ordered the animals to be taken on a short-cut to the circus grounds to save time. They were to walk down a deep gully rather than go over the proper railway crossing. Jumbo didn't like it. He lifted his heavy padded feet so slowly Tod wondered if they might miss the parade. But they made it on time and it proved to be the best parade of the season.

As the animals and performers marched back to the circus grounds, every act snapped quickly into place. The tents were up and waving gently in the early fall breeze. Cries of "Jumbo" were more frenzied than usual and Jumbo responded with his loudest trumpet of the summer as he entered the colossal, jammed tent arena.

Tod knew that there was only a brief time before the performance would begin, so he raced to the post box hoping for a letter from his mother. He was certain it would be there.

"Something for you," a clown called out and handed a thin envelope to Tod. It was a telegram, and when he opened it, Tod couldn't believe what he read.

Will arrive in New York on
September 1.

Mother

Such news deserved hoops and twirls in the
air, but Tod was startled from his thoughts when
a loud cry broke the silence.

"Tod, come here!" It was Jip. Something was
wrong.

Tod looked about. The circus was whirling
with action. He ran to Jip. The boy's face was
white.

"A beam fell on Arto. He's unconscious, and
they've taken him to the hospital. They have to
have someone at once to take his place in the
Café Act. Children are already calling for Tom
Thumb."

"I can do it," Tod couldn't help but shout. He
ran to find Fosset, who was sitting on his trunk
pondering the problem.

"Mr Fosset, please," Tod almost sobbed. "Let
me take Arto's place. I've watched the act every
day. I know just what to do, and Tom Thumb is
my friend."

Fosset looked over Tod's head and waved to
an older clown named Williams.

"Get ready to take Arto's place at once,
Williams." Fosset cried out. "Let one of Arto's
friends run through the Café Act with you.
We'll cancel your fire-engine show for tonight.
The audience is shouting for Tom Thumb."

Williams was not happy. He slumped through Clown Alley to look for a friend of Arto's.

Tod stood again in front of Fosset.

"I can do it," he pleaded. "Let me try."

"Don't bother me now, Tod. Can't you see I have a lot to do? Find your place near the centre ring and take care of Jumbo."

"But Mr Scott will be with him this evening." Tod tugged at Fosset's sleeve.

The clown leader brushed him aside and hurried towards Williams.

Tod sat down beside Williams's trunk. Grease paint, brushes and costumes were scattered about in total disarray. The middle-aged clown was known to be disorganized with his things, but he never missed a cue in the circus ring. Children laughed uproariously when he crashed his fire engine into a make-believe fire.

Tod began daubing white paint over his face and neck. It seemed to be what he had to do. His father had been a white-faced clown. Tod remembered that he had smiling black lines for a mouth and drooping eyes and a single black eyebrow. He drew them on his white painted face, just as he remembered. In the bottom of Williams's trunk he found a red wig. He put it on backwards. He saw an old coat with baggy sleeves slung over the back of the trunk. Tod pulled it over his shirt. A pair of oversized red boots completed his outfit.

Tod felt better under the painted face and ridiculous costume. He felt a little as if he somehow had his father with him again. He felt free. He wouldn't have to apologize for jumping and twisting through the air inside these clothes. He was a real clown at last and he could somersault and cartwheel whenever he pleased. He laughed. He twirled and swayed and began dancing a jig. People gathered around him and laughed with him. He spotted a grand piano and bench thirty feet apart and began pushing the piano towards the bench to get them together.

Fosset appeared.

"What have we here?" he asked.

"A new clown! A new face!" the other clowns shouted.

"I'm Tolliver—the Tumbling Clown," Tod cried.

"Well, Tod," Fosset said, laughing and trying to be serious at the same time. "You've won. Go out into the ring with Tom Thumb and do your best. I - I made a mistake. And, Williams, you can do your own routine as usual."

Tom Thumb and Tod ran to the centre ring. Jumbo and Scotty were sitting not far from them. Jumbo recognized Tod under his make-up and waved his trunk. The children in the tiers of seats around them screamed and cheered.

"I'm doing this for my mother," Tod said to

the tiny elephant beside him.

For a hundred performances Tod had watched the Café Act and had pretended he was the waiter. He knew every move. He made only one change. In the last scene, he balanced the tray on the top of his head and juggled three bottles in his hands. Tom Thumb grabbed one of them from the air. The crowd cheered. They wanted more.

Tod and Tom Thumb bowed again and again.

Fosset appeared as they left the arena.

"Congratulations to you, Tod," he shook the boy's hand. "Next season we may put you in the Café Act with Tom Thumb permanently. I've seen Arto and he'll recover. When he does, he says he wants to join the high-wire performers. So there may be a place for you."

Tod didn't know what to say. His mother was coming and now he might finally be a clown in the circus. He wondered if he could hold any more good news inside.

18

Lanterns now lit the road from the circus grounds to the railway station, for it had grown dark. A whistle blew. It was time to board the circus train.

Tod ran to join Jumbo, Tom Thumb and Scotty. He felt happily tired. His clown act with Tom Thumb had gone well. Jumbo had been magnificent. His opening trumpet had seemed to shake the tent.

As Tod walked out of doors towards the railway station, the warm summer night added to his blissful contentment. But he felt a little irritated when he joined Scotty, Tom Thumb and Jumbo to find that they had to walk along the tracks in such a narrow passage between the gully and a waiting passenger train that blocked their entrance to the circus train on the other side.

"If the beasts would go through the gully we wouldn't 'ave to walk around this bloomin' train," Scotty grumbled.

Jumbo waved his trunk in Tod's direction and Tod wrapped his arm around it.

Then without warning, a screeching whistle exploded into the peaceful sky. Scotty, Tod and the elephants turned around abruptly towards the sound. The flashing headlights of an oncoming train were heading directly towards them! Jumbo tightened his hold on Tod's arm and Scotty grabbed Tom Thumb around the neck.

An alarmed engineer ran from the train station. He raced down the tracks towards the roaring train, waving a flag.

"This is an unscheduled train!" he shouted. "It's not on the regular timetable!"

"Quick, Jumbo—Tom Thumb—Tod—down into the gully," Scotty ordered.

But the elephants refused to go.

Inside the unscheduled train, which was running at full speed, the engineer reacted with horror. He had no orders to stop in St Thomas. Yet in front of him loomed a waving flag, a crowd of people and a huge grey figure that blocked his track.

The engineer grabbed the whistle pulley, which blew three frantic blasts. He threw his engine into reverse. Brakemen in each car were ordered to lock the wheels but the train was not fitted with a modern braking system. It needed time to slow down. Sparks like giant firecrackers shot off the spinning wheels of steel into the dark night.

"Run, Jumbo! Run, Tom Thumb!" Tod screamed as he raced beside the terrified animals. Because they refused to go down the gully, they had to reach the end of the passenger train and cross in front of it to get to safety.

But their speed was no match for the oncoming train. It roared into Tom Thumb first and threw him down the embankment. Scotty and Tod jumped aside into the narrow space beside the waiting passenger train. Jumbo was too large to escape. There was a shaking thud, like the smashing of heavy metal into a mountainside. Jumbo was hit. His giant body stopped the train and tipped it to one side. Sparks again showered through the dark and the first boxcar ran off the tracks.

Tom Thumb lay in a ditch with a broken leg. Scotty and Tod were unhurt. But Jumbo was badly injured. A mighty roar rose from his throat. Then he rolled quietly onto his side. His trunk sought Scotty's hand, and in a few moments he was dead.

Everyone in the railway yard and on the circus train realized at once what had happened. A hush fell over the scattered group of people. They seemed to have turned into statues, posing just as they were when the accident happened, with terror and shock on all their faces.

Tod's reaction at first was disbelief. He wanted to rush to his friend and help lift him to his feet. Then he saw Scotty still holding Jumbo's trunk. He was sobbing uncontrollably.

But Tod couldn't cry. There weren't enough tears inside him to express his sorrow. He couldn't speak. Words weren't enough to tell of his hurt and shock.

Instead, he sat down on the railway track, his head buried in his hands. Every part of his body hurt. He wondered if his heart was bleeding with the pain that seemed to stab it every time he took a breath.

How could he leave his best friend in the world? He looked at the huge limp body lying beside the railway tracks. This wasn't the Jumbo he knew. His Jumbo was jolly and mischievous. His Jumbo was always there to listen to his troubles and pat his back with his long, swinging trunk when he was lonely. His Jumbo loved him.

Sounds of moving carts, and roaring animals and the barking orders of the manager loading the circus train could be heard. If the train didn't leave on schedule, there might be another accident.

Memories of Jumbo drifted through Tod's mind. There was the time when his mother was taken to the workhouse and Jumbo had listened to his sad story and drawn in close to Tod.

"He always made me feel better when he listened," Tod whispered aloud.

He smiled when he remembered all the hats

that Jumbo had whisked from his head.

Tod looked at Scotty again. He was still holding Jumbo's trunk. For a moment Tod thought of his father. When he had died, the loss had seemed so great to Tod that he thought all of life had ended. Now he remembered his father, the clown, with fondness and laughter. He realized that he would always have memories of Jumbo too.

Suddenly Tod smiled: he had forgotten his mother. She was in New York City and he would see her soon.

Tod stood straight and tall and saluted his friend Jumbo. He closed his eyes and Jumbo appeared in his mind, standing proud, his enormous trunk unfurled into the sky. If it hadn't been for Jumbo, Tod realized suddenly, he would never have become a real clown in the "Greatest Show on Earth."

"The show must go on," Tod began to murmur with the rhythm of the chugging locomotive. He walked slowly to the circus train and boarded the clown car.

EPILOGUE

Jumbo died on September 15, 1885. His death saddened people everywhere, for he was called "a pet of thousands and a friend of all." He was not just the largest living elephant in captivity during his lifetime, he was a zoo and circus celebrity. Wherever he went, both children and adults flocked to see him. Even the great French composer, Claude Debussy, wrote a piano piece and called it "Jimbo's Lullaby." He misspelled Jumbo's name, but refused to change it.

At the time of Jumbo's death, his measurements, as recorded by his owner, P.T. Barnum, were:

length in all—14 feet;

height to shoulder—12 feet;

weight—7 tons.

After Jumbo's death, a new word was added to the dictionary, meaning larger than normal or anything in which size is a virtue. People today fly in Jumbo Jets and eat Jumbo Burgers.

On the one-hundredth anniversary of Jumbo's death in 1985, the good people of St Thomas, Ontario erected a life-size statue of Jumbo, who gave his final performance in their town.

NOTES

The story of Jumbo is based on true facts, although chronology has been adjusted several times for the sake of the story. Scotty, Mr Bartlett and P.T. Barnum were real people and most of the events involving them, the London Zoo and the circus did happen. Only Tod and Molly Tolliver's story is fiction.

The song on page 41 was taken from "Walking in the Zoo" by Sweny and Lee, Hopewell and Crew, London, England, 1867.

On page 91, the quotation "A trophy of triumph . . ." is taken from the book *Jumbo* by W.P. Jolly, page 57.

On page 91 the song, "Jumbo said to Alice . . ." is taken from *The Ark in the Park* by Wilfred Blunt, page 181.

The poem on page 92 is found in the book *Jumbo* by Jolly, page 60, 61.

Books that were valuable
in writing Jumbo's story.

Among the Elephants, by Iain and Oria Douglas-Hamilton. The Viking Press, New York, 1975.

Animals in the Wild—Elephant, by Mary Hoffman. Random House, New York, 1984.

The Ark in the Park—The Zoo in the 19th Century, by Wilfrid Blunt. Tryon Gallery, London, England and Hamilton, Ontario, 1976.

Barnum's Own Story: The Autobiography of P.T. Barnum. Dover Publications, Inc., New York, 1961.

Circus! From Rome to Ringling, by Marian Murray. Greenwood Press, Westport, Conn., 2nd edition, 1975.

Circus Shoes, by Noel Streatfield. Dell Publishing Co. Inc., New York, 1985.

Elephants, the Vanishing Giants, by Don Freeman. G.P. Putnam Sons, New York, 1981.

Here Comes the Circus, by Peter Verney. Paddington Press, New York, 1978.

Jumbo, by W.P. Jolly. Constable, London, 1976.

Jumbo—The Biggest Elephant in All the World, by Florence McLaughlin Burns. Scholastic-TAB, Richmond Hill, Ontario, 1978.

London's Zoo, by Gwynne Vevers. The Bodley Head, London, 1977.

The Story of Jumbo, by W.F.L. Edwards. Elgin County Pioneer Museum, St Thomas, Ontario, 1985.

Tequila the African Elephant, by Judy Ross. D.C. Heath Canada Ltd., Toronto, 1978.